An Age of Treason

PARTS ONE AND TWO

WALTER SCHMIDT

Fulton Books
Meadville, PA

Published by Fulton Books 2023

ISBN 979-8-88982-605-7 (paperback)
ISBN 979-8-89221-208-3 (hardcover)
ISBN 979-8-88982-607-1 (digital)

Printed in the United States of America

AUTHOR'S NOTE

On June 15, 1215, a document sealed by King John of England made promises to his subjects that would assure justice and freedoms. Known as the Magna Carta, it formed the basis of law in England and those countries influenced by English tradition.

The Magna Carta (Latin for "great chart") alluded to in this account is a series of clauses or articles prescribed by a clandestine group to undermine the intent of the US Constitution, establish an elite class to manage the country, and subject the general population to a life of subservience to the state in the name of social justice.

This missive is presented as a chronicle (i.e., a fictional record of happenings in the order in which they happened and not always narrated in any particular literary style).

Treason, according to the Constitution, is an act that reflects a deliberate attempt to overthrow the government. It also infers aid and comfort to the enemy. In this account, not only are the belligerents intending an overthrow of a free democratic system but, by their actions, they are also inviting aid and comfort to the socialist and communist enemies of our nation and a distortion of our way of life.

PART 1

A Hidden Agenda
Revealed

CHAPTER 1

The Beginning

People often wonder how politicians come into their sometimes lifetime careers in the public arena. Some do by wanting to make a difference, assisting their fellow man against the excesses of human nature, business, or government, to better everyone's way of life as servants to the people. Some do by wanting to achieve an ideological goal in the governance of people to realize power and, in the process, gain great financial security. And then there are those like Cecil Howard who start out born into financial security and wealth and seek the grandeur of living in the limelight of personal power.

Born to wealth, Cecil had all the privileges of a rich family. Never an ethical man, most of his father's work was acquired primarily through graft and corruption. Payoff was the marketing strategy employed, and he made every attempt to use any and all means to influence those in political office to direct major public projects to his company. Acquiring millions of dollars over time, he bought off attorneys and even judges to protect his considerable empire. Now he had the opportunity to thrust his son into a political arena that could bring him even more influence.

Cecil never lived in the real world. Raised in luxury and educated at a prestigious college, his father lived in hopes that his son would have a distinctive job in politics upon his graduation from school. However, like many of his classmates from that era, Cecil decided he wanted to join the military first and be part of the war's end, then raging as World War II. Unlike other second lieutenants of that period, who would be thrown in the war fronts, he had hoped he would have the privilege of working at the Pentagon. His father would see to that. Through political connections, the elder Howard succeeded in persuading his political cronies to get Cecil a "cushy desk job" or, at the very worst, a staff assignment in a war zone, not too close to any forward area. Like it or not, Cecil got the war zone assignment as a general staff aide in a Pacific-command area. Known by his father's influential contacts, Cecil was looked upon as untouchable. So instead of hazardous duty, Lt. Howard spent his tour of duty arranging cocktail parties for the senior brass and wheeling and dealing political favors for junior officers, far from any front. It was not uncommon for him to create liaisons for junior or senior brass when it came to the opposite sex since he acquired full knowledge of who the players were. He too never let a dalliance for himself get by him. His power to seduce women took on an art form.

After the war, Cecil entered formal politics. Having tasted the fruits of the power of manipulation and self-gratification in his small role in the military, the world of national politics suited him just fine. With his dad's money and political associations, running for political office came easy. Coupled with his military background to which he exaggerated his accomplishments, not only did he win his first run for office but he also had no trouble solidifying his base. He became so enamored with his newfound power that one day, he thought he might become one of the next presidents of the United States. Besides, he was just beginning to realize that only in America was there unlimited opportunity. And he came to the awakening that this country was constructed on sound principles. We are what we are because the Constitution laid out the framework for what is now one of the freest nations on earth.

Cecil Howard was sitting in the Oval Office, contemplating his current set of predicaments. Just coming off a grueling campaign and, finally, the inauguration events, he was now confronted by two major problems. His party, the Citizens Progressive Populist Party (C3P), had launched him into the election on the promise that he would follow an agenda that he was having difficulty coming to terms with. The other was his own personal demon, his many affairs with other women, and keeping this separated from his new public image. Not to mention keeping the First Lady from being a constant nag regarding her suspicions about these liaisons. It was bad enough to have to deal with affairs of state without facing a wife who was constantly belittling you about your indiscretions. She knew that if she became too vocal about her suspicions, the media would pick it up, and there would be scandal all around. His only hope was that she liked the limelight she was now in and won't upset the apple cart.

Cecil was a party loyalist, and the Citizens Progressive Populist Party's new chairman was intent on beginning the process of integrating a plan that the party, up until now, was unable to implement. But, with their party in as the new administration and in control of both houses, the wheels could begin to turn.

The C3P had long held the view that it was going to be necessary to socialize America. Ever since the Roosevelt administration came into office, the economic advisors and power brokers of that era saw that the C3P could attain almost absolute power, if they set upon a long-term plan to moderate the original intentions of the Constitution, direct the thinking of Americans, and grow government into the absolute caretaker of all. Was there a meaning in a party whose acronym CPPP just happened to be similar in fashion to the Russian acronym of CCCP for Union of Soviet Socialist Republics? And what about CCP for China Communist Party? Cecil, however, was having trouble with this ideal. First, he did not like the communists as a matter of principle and perfect socialism was their goal. Secondly, he felt that though Americans deserved the best the country had to offer, he wasn't sure a master plan to socialize America was the answer. And to some extent, based on the rhetoric from the zealous portrayers of this movement, he wasn't too sure as to whether or not some of what they wanted to do was treasonous.

So while sipping his favorite aperitif on the rocks, he concluded he would play it cool. He would settle into the new role he was now playing, nix the extracurricular female activity for an interim, and see just what his party had in mind for implementing their plan during his watch. It wasn't long before he found out.

Sam Butford was a crusty old coot with many years serving in the Senate. As vice president, this was his first opportunity to enter one of the highest offices in the land, and he was relishing it. Having buttered the bread of loyal supporters through legislative action and influence, he now saw the opportunity to implement, along with his activist associates of political maneuvering, the C3P agenda of putting into place the acquisition of ultimate power.

Sam had wanted to be the candidate for president, but his party convinced him that the popular vote of the people would not accept him as readily as Cecil Howard. Cecil had the charisma, the style, and the force of speech that seemed legitimate to the citizens of the country. And that is exactly what they were missing in prior elections and what contributed to their losses. Sam Butford was experienced, but he just didn't have the charisma. But, as they convinced Sam, he would be the perfect backup to Cecil Howard if their agenda was not going to be followed, for they had a plan for even that.

The C3P was right in their approach, for Cecil Howard did win the election on his charm and speech, narrowly defeating his opponent. Without his style, they would have lost.

Underlying the C3P was a very secret clique of four very wealthy individuals. Born to riches, none of them ever worked a day in their life involving physical labor. All Ivy League, educated at their benefactor's expense, they evolved to a position where they could pursue their ideals. The ideal that most enthralled them was that of the acquisition of power through the pursuit of a socialist America. They concluded that average Americans are not smart enough to look after themselves and that America as a socialist nation must look after them. But, in the accomplishment of that ideal, there was the opportunity of building a system that would put huge power in the hands of the elite (politicians and bureaucrats) using the population as the means to their end.

On a cold evening in January, a black sedan wound its way up a secluded road in the Adirondack Mountains. About an hour and a half's drive from Albany, a private cabin of some size, surrounded by a security fence and guarded twenty-four hours a day by a special group of security personnel, was outlined against the glimmer of a mountain lake. An imposing figure was behind the wheel, and he was pondering tonight's special meeting. As he drove up to the gate, a guard with pistol at his side stopped the vehicle. Upon recognition, the gate was opened, and the vehicle was allowed through. The driver motored up to the front of the cabin. Lights were on inside, and three other vehicles were parked at the front of the building. The mysterious individual stepped from the car. The air was crisp and clear. There was very little snow on the ground, and the crunch of this portly figure's steps echoed in the brisk night air. As he entered the cabin, three figures were settled in chairs around a heavy table. It was obvious that this was going to be an ominous and a sinister meeting.

The three sitting at the table, along with the latest arrival, constituted this ignominious and very secret group. They each occupied a position of specialty and used a code to refer to themselves and to imply their specialty. C1 was the chairman and had established and carried out all administrative and organizational issues. C2 was responsible for gathering intelligent information, promoting propaganda or smear campaigns, including "character destruction" or "character liquidation." C3 was responsible for implementation or integration of people, places, and things into the American environment that would turn popular belief from a democratic republic to socialism. C4 was the acquirer of money through whomever and whatever. No stone would be unturned to acquire cash for this massive endeavor, legal or illegal.

C1, code name "Ivan," was a clever, well-educated man, six feet and four inches tall, and 250 pounds. Not necessarily handsome, he exuded dominance. He had few scruples, was used to free living, and was divorced. He never had any children. Like the rest of the group, he never was in the limelight, so it was easy for him to be totally clandestine. With a family that had a great deal of wealth, C1 entered the financial world after graduating from college. Armed with resources of capital, he started to play in the realm of international currency trading. Gifted with powers of foresight and a penchant for the exhilaration of risk, he managed to parlay risky investments into riches of his own in massive proportions. However, after accomplishing this, he needed a new challenge. The idea of great power and the ability to manipulate people instead of money became his new addiction.

C2, code name Casper, was a wiry, somewhat anemic-looking individual. He was short in stature and suffered greatly from "small man's disease," that stigma of needing to prove you're bigger than you really are. Always trying to prove something, he was a master at deception. Also, as an admirer of the intelligence network of the Third Reich, he sought out every piece of information he could find that would reveal the inner workings of the world's intelligence systems. He even tried to get into the CIA. Unfortunately, background checks prevented him from any consideration. It seemed he had some questionable dealings with political figures in his hometown who sued him for libel and won.

Disappointed in his efforts to get into the US intelligence community, he studied the KGB intelligence machine of Soviet Russia. Plying undercover strategies, he developed a network of paid informants to help him uncover the dirty laundry of actors, actresses, politicians, underworld figures, and heavyweight business CEOs. Once armed with scandalous information, he got his thrills by blackmail. By contractual arrangements, he would uncover personal secrets about individuals to either "dish the dirt" or to allow vengeance to play out between underworld figures. Since money was the least of his worries, he did it for the thrill of it all. Now with an opportunity to work with a clandestine group with higher ambitions, he had the opportunity to thrive on finding, planning, and implementing all the necessities of his specialty. Applying his talents to an ideology made it so much more gratifying.

C3, code name "Merlin," was an anomaly. Of average build and intelligence, he had a suave and charming personality. Underneath, however, he was a devious and threatening character. It's amazing how the innate characteristics of an individual can make the difference in how persuasive one person can be compared to another. This was C3's forte. As evil personified, he brought his cunning instincts to each of "The Committee's" planned pursuits.

Living off his family fortune, he had spent most of his time moving among the "beautiful people." From Hollywood to the Hamptons, he lived life by frolicking through the rich and the famous, careful never to become too close to anyone. As a favor to others or to avenge his own inclinations, he had the ability to hurt people in serious ways. C3 could do it cleanly without a trace to himself. Cold as ice underneath, he could convince others on how to severely destroy people or he could present a facade of compassion and caring. Able to switch between each extreme, one never knew where his real intents would lie. This gave him a style of intimidation that even the strongest of character would submit. Through these traits, he could find the ways and means to distort opinions or destroy a person's career at will.

C4, code name "Juno" (named after the mythical Roman goddess and guardian of the finances), was the only woman in this sinister ensemble. Somewhat attractive but extraordinarily sharp, she had an accounting, economic, and financial mind. She had worked in the big financial houses of Wall Street and had strong inner knowledge of the systems, both national and international. Bored with the capitalistic system, she felt that there was a way to control wealth on a massive scale. Through a government-controlled mechanism, socialism would fill that possibility. Because of her knowledge of the players of the nation and the world, she now had the ability to not only be instrumental in sourcing funds but to also contribute in ways that could force the country into liberalizing economic policies to nefarious ends, thus paving the way to expediting the incorporation of various entities into nationalized programs.

C1 had met C4 in the financial world, and they had come to know each other's ideology as being similar. They complimented each other's talents and knew they could form a viable relationship.

It doesn't matter as how C2 and C3 became part of this group, but they did. What was important was that their contributions were invaluable to the outcome of historical events.

Ivan was the last to arrive at the meeting. Glaring at the group, he inquired as to whether anyone had trouble keeping their trip secret. All replied there was no way anyone knew they either were gone or where they were going.

Ivan responded by saying: "Good! We must accomplish a great deal tonight and be back to our normal activities tomorrow as though we were never gone. We must maintain our anonymity. No one must ever know who we are or what we do as 'The Committee.'"

This was the first time the term was used to describe the group. It was to become the conscience of C3P in all matters and woe to the party member who failed to carry out his place within the party according to what would soon be a prescription for subtle and eventually massive turmoil in the American political landscape.

However, The Committee would never be known individually by anyone within the C3P. Ivan then proceeded to proclaim: "Tonight, we are going to solidify an agenda so profound and so effective that it will change America to our liking. This declaration, the Magna Carta to convert America to a socialist nation, is to be named our 'Articles of Acquisition.' We will implement each article one by one over time through several administrations until full acquisition of our ideal occurs." Ivan paced the floor, gathering his thoughts. "So to begin the process, we will start with article 1: 'The end will justify the means in all matters.' That is, any action necessary to reach an objective will be utilized, whether or not it is traditionally amoral or immoral. The end is the all-important factor to accomplish the intended mission."

The Committee proceeded to work all through the night, establishing all the Articles of Acquisition. By sunrise, they had created a plan that even Satan himself would consider a masterpiece.

CHAPTER 2

A Fateful Decision

Cecil Howard was now in office for three months. Even though World War II had only ended fifteen years earlier, the world was living out new fears. Russia was now a great power with nuclear capability, and they were preparing to have a physical presence in the West. Trouble was occurring in the Far East, and America was being drawn into it. All these issues were pressing him greatly. So, to relieve his tensions, he sought out the two things that eased his physical and mental anguish: a dalliance with one of his favorite interests and pain killer to ease the constant throb in his back. Years earlier, during football practice, Cecil was injured; he never got over the effects. It had become routine to use his favorite pain killer to ease the hurt. At 10:00 p.m., while a guard was distracted, Cecil slipped out through a White House gate, jumped into a waiting car, and sped off to an undisclosed hotel.

Cecil's wife was looking for her husband to find out what was on tomorrow's schedule. For some reason, she could not find him.

So she asked one of the staff members. "Do you know where the president is?"

"Ah no, ma'am, I'm not sure. But he's probably attending some secret late evening meeting of state and probably will return shortly."

She, however, had the feeling that he might be up to his old self. So she inquired again. "It's not likely that the president would just take off. Surely he must have told someone he had a meeting?"

The staff, suitably emplaced by the C3P to watch the goings in the White House, had their suspicions as to what he might be up to because at all times, they also needed to know where he was.

"Well, ma'am, I'm sure he must have told someone. I just don't know who. Perhaps, the chief of staff knows."

The staff member clearly was trying not to look the First Lady in the eye for fear she might read too much in the sheepish look on his face. The First Lady stomped off to look for the chief of staff.

The White House staff had noticed the president was not acting himself lately. He seemed to go through periods of being "on" and then "off." As to this incident, no more was thought of it, and by morning, the president was back in the Oval Office as usual, showing nothing different in his demeanor. That, however, did not keep his wife from asking.

"Where were you last night?"

"What do you mean?" was his reply.

"You know what I mean. I asked everybody here where you were, and no one knew. Are you seeing someone again? Who is it this time?"

The president, now looking to make sure there was no staff in the area, said, "Why are you asking me this? It's not what you think. I have sensitive issues that come up unannounced, and when I have to go, I go."

"I'm not talking about you going to the bathroom and taking a leak. I'm talking about seeing your outside female interests. What broad is it now? I thought we talked this all out before you ran for president, and you assured me you were done with that sort of thing. I'm telling you I will not go through that all over again! If you start, this time, I'll blow the lid off!"

"Oh, come on, honey, don't be like that. It's over. I just had some late business of state that was hush-hush, that's all. Next time, I'll be sure to let you know I'm going." He hoped she would buy this story.

"Well, just know if it happens again, I'll have it looked into. I still don't trust you."

Things were increasingly troublesome in the Far East. By late summer, it was obvious; more military advisors would be required if any hope was to be given to the civilian regime now in power. But, through constant micromanaging by the White House and Congress over the progress of this conflict, the military could not establish sensible missions or projections of where the American position should be in resolving the issues. It just continued to deteriorate. President Howard couldn't get excited over the Far East mess since his immediate attention was focused on Russia. The chance of nuclear weapons being situated near American shores was looking imminent. Also, he was suddenly aware that there was a force behind the C3P, his party, that was going to be calling the shots politically, and he didn't like it. The party chairman was going to be meeting with him to outline an agenda of far-reaching proportions, and the president was going to be obligated to begin turning the wheels to achieve all the stated objectives. What bothered him the most was the utter secrecy involved and the clandestine nature by which the C3P wanted their intentions to occur whatever they were.

*****

John Bugman, the new party chairman, was an ambitious and driven character. Making senior class chairman in college, he thrived in the role of "little tin god." After that, he always sought after a leadership role so he could dwell in an aura of power. Involvement in the C3P was exactly the role he felt he was destined for, and he flourished in supporting and working for the election of many key public figures. Of course, he didn't always follow all the rules to get his candidates to where they needed to be, but credibility was not one of John's major attributes. Being extremely liberal, he bent all the rules and let the chips fall where they may. He could always use his guile to outwit his opponent's interjections of suspicions or challenges. For that reason, John Bugman had been selected by the C3P to be the new party chairman.

The Committee was ready to force their influence on the C3P and to make it implement the tenets of its new charter. To do this, it was time to confront John Bugman and to incorporate him into the mantra of total commitment to the Articles of Acquisition. Since The Committee was totally clandestine, even John Bugman would not know who the individuals of The Committee were, but he would meet them.

The Committee developed an elaborate courier system whereby, through the use of written messages, couriers would pick up the messages dropped in bus and train station lockers and deliver them to the intended recipient. John Bugman received his invitation by courier. When the courier arrived at John's apartment, John was taken aback by receiving a courier-delivered message. He was immediately intrigued. The invitation stated in simple form that he was invited to meet some very important people who held in their hands financial and political power of great magnitude, and he could be a part of it. To be at this meeting, he should be outside his apartment at 8:00 p.m., where a black sedan would pick him up and take him to an undisclosed hotel. John was somewhat suspicious but at the same time very curious. He decided that the message's form of delivery and the statement of financial and political power were enough to convince him that this was a meeting he needed to see through.

So, at the appointed time, he stepped out of his apartment, and almost immediately, the black sedan appeared. Hesitant at first, he almost changed his mind. Giving in to his curiosity, he stepped into the vehicle and settled into the back seat. The driver said nothing. John tried to make small talk, but the driver did not respond. After thirty minutes of driving, the driver pulled over to the curb where another person was standing. Thinking that this individual was going to the meeting as well, John was surprised to see the driver step out of the sedan, and the other individual took over the driving, leaving the former driver to walk off into the night. The new driver then stated that his name was Randy and that he would be bringing him to the meeting spot. It would be about an hour's drive, and he should make himself comfortable. He offered him a thermos, which contained a triple vodka martini on the rocks with a twist of lemon. John felt that this indeed would be a comfortable ride.

The hotel was obviously upscale. The meeting was to be in a suite on the seventh floor. Escorted by the driver, John was taken to the designated room. The driver already had a door key and let John in and immediately departed. As John entered the room, he could only see four dark figures at a table. The whole situation was starting to seem like an old black-and-white movie drama. John was instructed to stop where he was at and to take a seat. The lighting in the room was directed at John, so he could not see any of the figures. They told him to relax, this was to take some time, and that arrangements were made for him to be returned to his apartment at the completion of the meeting.

Ivan began. "John, you have the privilege of participating in something so vast and so encompassing that your ambitions will be beyond your wildest dreams. To what we are about to offer, you will have to commit yourself completely in this historical endeavor. Consider carefully your response because this is an offer you can't refuse. Your acceptance of this meeting invitation has locked you into a relationship that you cannot break. Let's just say that anything other than your complete acceptance means your permanent termination."

John felt a shiver pass through his body. Curiously, he didn't know if it was fear or the exhilaration at the thought of an opportunity of a lifetime. He heard himself say "I accept."

Ivan then proceeded to explain. "I repeat. This is a lifetime commitment. John, you have just obligated yourself to complete obedience to this committee. We will now convey to you the precepts of our mission, and you will retain a copy of this charter in your safe at the C3P headquarters office. It will be referred to as confirming evidence of our strategy only on an a needed basis to selected individuals at our direction. Guard this document at all cost and never let it get into the wrong hands. Should it become public information, it could have serious consequences, particularly to you."

John responded, "How can this document create such a problem? What does it represent?"

Ivan then began with the first article, and other committee members added their comments as each article was related to John. When Ivan was finished, John drew a deep breath and fell back in his chair.

John, with a hesitant voice, said, "Not...ah...only is this overwhelmingly all-inclusive but it also clearly—well, it seems to me that it indicates that...maybe...many—that is, many could consider the acts of this committee and all the C3P as…ah…well, what I want to say is we could be complicit in possible acts of treason."

Ivan blurted out, "Nonsense! If we handle this properly, our actions will be looked upon as in the best interest of the people of this country. By their acceptance and their votes, they will still democratically vote in an increasingly socialistic system."

Clever! And he, John, could be part of a powerful organization. He was just ambitious enough to accept all these.

The meeting concluded, Randy, the driver, was summoned, and John Bugman was delivered back to his apartment with instructions to set up a meeting with the president. The president needed to be firmly behind the program, and John Bugman was to see that Cecil Howard was ready to move forward with the C3P agenda.

*****

At the direction of The Committee and with the Articles of Acquisition locked in his briefcase, John Bugman headed for the White House for his scheduled meeting with the president. John wasn't sure how the president would react to the articles, but he knew there was no turning back. The president was going to accept them or the first article would be implemented to accomplish the party and The Committee's agenda.

Arriving at the White House, John was ushered into the Oval Office where the president was waiting. As John entered the room, the president was pacing the floor.

"John, I don't like any of this," he uttered. "Since when does a force behind the C3P dictate what's going to be done in this country? It goes beyond all reason as to why I should be part of all this."

"Mr. President, you know that it is impossible to fight a force that is so well structured and organized as The Committee. Backed by huge wealth, they have the ability to create or destroy. You wouldn't be president had they not been behind you. And let me tell you there isn't anything they don't know about you personally and professionally. The C3P is making the move to implement a strategy put forth by The Committee, and I am here to let you see the charter that is to be used to accomplish our ends. Reserve your frustrations until I have laid all this before you." John sincerely hoped the president would be on board.

Flustered, the president said, "Well, all right! But this had better be good."

John set the briefcase on the table and removed the articles. John explained the extreme secrecy under which these articles must be kept. He then proceeded to go over each article, watching the president's reaction after each one was read.

After they were all reviewed, the president stood up.

"In all my years of political life, I never expected to be involved in something so all-encompassing as this! It brings deep dread to my very being and a fear for the destiny of a country I so deeply love. I can't take it all in. It's more than I can fathom right now."

At this response, John reminded the president that his personal life (alluding to his affairs) hadn't been all that stellar.

"You understand, Mr. President, that you have a lot to lose, if you fail to unite with the party in this effort."

"Oh, so it comes to that, doesn't it?" Now the president was visibly angry. "I am well aware of my personal indiscretions, but that does not mean I have lost my love for the freedom only this country has to offer."

"It's not only that, Mr. President. It's much more. Read the first article and either you will join this effort or something more serious than simple blackmail will occur."

The president slumped into his chair.

"Leave me, John. I need to absorb this. It's not an easy change for me to make. Do I want C3P to dominate the future of my country? Yes, I do. Do I want to commit to complete socialism? I have to think it out."

John, knowing the president was ambivalent, said, "Call me when you are ready to talk more. Don't take too long. The Committee needs to know you are fully on board."

With that, John left.

When John left the White House security gate, immediately, a black sedan intercepted him. Randy was driving, and he dropped the window and told John to get in. He hopped into the car, and they sped off. Randy said they were headed to another meeting with The Committee. It was obvious; The Committee wanted to know the president's attitude and response.

Arriving at a different upscale hotel, an hour from the capitol, John entered the suite. Again, the room was darkened, lighting in his direction, and the shadowy figures were sitting at the table.

Ivan then proceeded to ask, "How did the president react?"

John, knowing that his answer was not going to be to their liking, said, "He's very nervous about the whole situation. I can say that if you think he is going to accept the articles, it is my opinion that it is very doubtful. We will know soon."

That said, John left the meeting knowing that the answers given were not acceptable to The Committee. When he got back to his apartment, no sooner had he sat down to ponder all that was about to happen, the phone rang. Answering it, he was surprised to hear it was the president.

"John!" The president was clearly abrupt. "I am telling you that I will be the president of the people, and I will protect and defend the Constitution. Anything that is contrary to that will not take place during my watch. There is your answer!" And with that, he hung up.

It was now out of John's hands. The Committee would activate its intent.

Upon hearing about the president's response, Ivan called for a meeting at the mountain retreat. So, on a balmy summer night, deep in the mountains of the northeast, a meeting was convened to discuss a course of action.

CHAPTER 3

A Lethal Consideration

"It's obvious that we have a president in office that will obstruct our ability to carry out the articles. We cannot wait three and a half years or seven plus years to start this movement. I am also concerned about what appears to be the start of a breakdown in the president's mental and physical state. He's been erratic in his demeanor, and our key staff people say he is not always himself. We cannot take a chance on what we originally thought was a good choice. Therefore, the president must be removed from office." Ivan was definite in his statements.

Merlin interjected, "Ivan, even if he's removed by forced resignation or if we conspire to expose him as unfit for office so that he's impeached, he's seen the articles, and therefore, he puts us and the party at risk."

Immediately, Casper jumped in, "There is no alternative. We must consider termination. We can accomplish this by creating an assassin. Leave it to me. In a matter of weeks, I will have it planned out, and upon your approval, we can carry it out without suspicion to ourselves or the C3P."

Ivan challenged, "Can you do it smart?"

"Yes!" Casper responded. This was followed by a hot debate related to the idea of termination, but in the end, they all agreed the first article needed to be implemented.

Ivan, with determination in his face, blurted, "Casper, get started! Meeting adjourned!"

Casper examined the president's background carefully, especially his political and, where possible, personal movements over the past several years. From early on, it seemed that any time Cecil Howard had traveled to various cities on his political junkets, he never was without a female companion and not always his wife. On one such particular trip to Chicago, though he started out with no obvious companion, he was invited to a dinner with one of the prominent underworld figures. This individual had a girlfriend of significant beauty, and during the dinner, Cecil managed to make an acquaintance that developed into an affair, much to the displeasure of this local godfather. The affair was ended quickly by two very healthy bodyguards confronting Cecil and telling him the error of his ways. The local godfather never got over it. He hoped one day he could have a reason to wreak revenge upon Cecil Howard.

Ironically, Casper knew this underworld figure. He had used the godfather's organization to influence voting in that state. It looked like this offered an opportunity, and Casper made note of it in his plan book. Casper now set upon a plan to select an individual who would remove the intended victim. The questions to be answered were who, what, where, how, and how to make it all look like a random act. First, though, who will carry it out? Enter Bobby Adams.

Bobby Adams grew up in Chicago. His family situation was a troubled one. His father drank excessively, and his mother soon divorced him when Bobby was just four years old. She never remarried and dedicated her life to caring for Bobby and scraping a living out of her modest environment. Not educated, she took menial tasks and managed to bring up her boy the best she could. She had a weak heart, and though it wasn't evident in the early years, her hardships made her condition worse. By the time Bobby graduated from high school, his mother had come to the end of her rope. She died of a heart attack suddenly in her sleep. All at once, Bobby was alone. His parents had not had close relatives, so, having nowhere to go, Bobby decided to enlist in the Army.

After boot camp, Bobby signed up for Special Forces. Qualifying as an expert marksman during his basic training, Bobby was encouraged to go to Sniper School. Upon completing his Special Forces and sniper training, Bobby was a natural to be chosen for an assignment in the Far East. In no time, he was serving in the conflict, first, as an advisor and then as an actual special task operative.

Being a sniper, serving in the jungle for extended periods of time, was a very stressful and depriving existence. The inky black nights, the oppressive heat, the humidity and persistent rain, the insects and deadly beasts of the jungle, and the presence of a ruthless enemy were enough to affect the most hardened of natures. Though Bobby found his niche in the Army, he still was affected by his repeated trips to the jungle, living like an isolated animal in the forest.

After a time, when Bobby got back from one of his missions and had taken leave, he was exposed to the opportunity of acquiring drugs. Encouraged by other Army buddies that the drugs could take the edge off, Bobby gave it a try. It would change him entirely. He started in a small way, even taking a small cache with him on his missions. He found it reduced his fear, and at least, at first, it seemed to heighten his senses. He thought it made him a more effective shooter. At this time, he had no trouble hitting a six-inch bull's-eye at five hundred yards.

The drugs were changing Bobby, and he would become moody. He began to get into arguments at the drop of a pin. One such time ended with him punching a senior enlisted man. Another time, he stabbed another soldier with a knife in the mess hall. It wasn't long. Suspecting that Bobby was a user, combined with his other serious infractions, Bobby was bounced out of the Army with a dishonorable discharge. He left the military bitter toward the Army and his country, both of which he thought had betrayed him.

Upon arriving stateside, Bobby soon found that his need for drugs was rearing its ugly head. By the time he got back to his hometown, he needed to find a local source to satisfy his habit. It wasn't long, and a local pusher provided him with his stuff. Living off Army pay that he had little use to spend in the Far East, he now was rapidly depleting his financial reserve. A source of money had to be found if he was to avoid the ravages of withdrawal. Unknowingly, his pusher would be instrumental in fixing him up with a contact that would end all his problems.

CHAPTER 4

A Lethal Task

Casper decided that the best place to carry out the task should be a site where the president would typically be present. There was to be a special event in late spring, spearheading off-year elections with a rally in Chicago at the lakefront. If planned right, this might be the right place at the right time. As soon as a task operative was determined, the rest of the planning could take place.

He now made arrangements to solicit the vengeful Chicago godfather and have him cough up a likely candidate. As it happened, the Chicago godfather controlled the drug market in the city and could find out pretty quickly the likely candidates for the job. Bobby Adams had revealed most of his background to his pusher, and his qualifications fit the intended job so well that Casper jumped on this opportunity as soon as Bobby was submitted. Bobby was not so far gone as a user, so he would still be effective.

Yet, addicted and short on funds, he could be enticed into carrying out a mission.

Casper arranged for a clandestine meeting by one of his agents with Bobby Adams. The pusher told Bobby that someone had a special job for him and was willing to pay $150,000. All he had to do to find out about it was to stand outside his apartment building at 10:00 p.m., and a black sedan would pick him up. Bobby did as he was instructed. One hundred fifty thousand dollars was too good an opportunity to pass up if it was real. By now, Bobby had few scruples and was willing to do almost anything to satisfy his physical needs.

He stepped out of his apartment in the inky black night. A flash of headlights suddenly appeared, and a black sedan pulled up. As he approached the car, the window opened, and the driver told him to get into the back seat. Bobby hopped in, and the car took off. The driver then proceeded to tell Bobby that he was selected for his special talents and that he was to eliminate a particular political figure. It wasn't important that Bobby know who the person was; in fact, it was preferable that he didn't know; it might be better for everybody. A clean, untraceable weapon would be made available and disposed of by his accomplice who would be his spotter. He did not have to worry about their escape route after the mission. That was planned, and he would never be found out. All he had to do was to wait for a message in his mailbox as to when he would be picked up as he was tonight. When that day came, he was to expect to be gone for two or three days. The money would be paid immediately upon completion of the task in cash.

All Bobby could think about was the $150,000 and what it would bring him. And what did he care about political figures? One less would be a good thing, considering his frame of mind. So he was fully for the idea. Besides, it might feel good to make a nice, clean shot fill his pockets with change, not to mention other goodies.

Casper presented his plan to The Committee. He said, "This task can occur at a political rally in Chicago, taking place at a lakefront park between Michigan Avenue and Lake Shore Drive." The date of the rally had already been set but not released for security reasons. "If The Committee agrees, we will affect a go, and things will automatically start into motion."

The Committee agreed. History would now be impacted.

On a rather balmy day in May, Bobby Adams received a message in the mail that he would be picked up that night. He was to take three days of clothes, toiletry items, and be prepared to spend some long afternoons preparing his program. The program was to zero his soon-to-be-provided sniper rifle, to hit a bull's-eye target from approximately 1,510 feet or just over five hundred yards.

When Bobby was picked up at the appointed hour, as it happened, the driver of the vehicle picking up Bobby was none other than the infamous Randy. Randy was to be the spotter. But, first, Randy brought Bobby to a hotel just across from the lakefront park, where the political rally was to be held. The room was already arranged for, so Bobby didn't have to check in. He simply walked up to the twentieth floor and entered a rather nice room facing the park.

Randy followed later and told Bobby, "Tomorrow, I'll be picking you up at nine in the morning. We have about an hour's drive into the country where there is a secluded rifle range. I will retain the rifle after each day's shooting, and it will be brought up to the hotel room only on the day of the event. I will expect that you will be in a relaxed condition to practice. When you are satisfied the weapon is zeroed, you will be brought back to your room where you will stay until the mission is completed. I will see to it that the weapon is brought to you by me on the day of the event so as to avoid any accidental exposure. Besides, Secret Service or police authorities may be in the area on the specific day because security will be heightened."

It only took one day's session for Bobby to zero the weapon. After approximately twelve separate groupings in the bull's-eye from five hundred yards out, all shots were within the diameter of a golf ball; Bobby was satisfied the weapon was on. Randy, spotting each shot through his spotting scope, couldn't help but be impressed by such marksmanship. Yes, wind could make a difference, and for the zeroing, there was none, but no matter, it was obvious Bobby was a crack shot. Now, if the day was a windless day when the task was carried out, the outcome would be obvious.

Bobby felt pretty good about his target practice. If all went well, his $150,000 was in the bag. So, once he was returned to his hotel, he prepared himself a fix and slid into a chair where a glassy stare and obvious sedated look came over him.

On the third day, Randy slipped into the room with the rifle under a raincoat. Also, he carried a tote bag filled with $100 bills, letting Bobby see the booty he was to be paid. Fortunately, the weather looked like rain, so Randy acquired little notice as he entered the hotel when he went up to Bobby's room. Looking out the window overlooking the park, a large platform was visible where the president was going to speak, and the podium was already set up, and people were moving about, preparing for the big event. Chairs were placed for important people on the platform. Bobby and Randy set up a desk at the window, and opening the window, they were able to place the weapon on the long end of the desk toward the center of the room. Bobby was able to place the rifle into his shoulder and rest the bipod of the rifle on the desk, and he could place the crosshairs of the scope dead on the podium. A worker at the platform, setting the microphone, briefly stepped up to the podium, and Bobby caught the worker in his crosshairs. Bobby knew if his victim stood at the podium, his chances for success were assured, barring any wind or weather considerations.

The hours went by, and the crowd in the park increased to large numbers. Several speakers addressed the crowd and huge shouts; whooping and laughter wafted through the afternoon air. As the day drew on, the weather continued to improve. It no longer looked like rain, and the wind, normally brisk coming off Lake Michigan, was barely a whim-

AN AGE OF TREASON

per. Then the crowd began to yell and clap as a motorcade of limousines drove up to the platform.

*****

Early that morning, before he went to Chicago, President Howard had breakfast with his wife. Making this trip was one of those things a president must do to satisfy his party and those constituents who looked forward to his helping them in their runs for office. On this particular morning, Cecil was loathing to make the trip. Looking at his wife across the table, she was wearing her nightdress, and her hair was hanging freely onto her shoulders. For some reason, it was many a year that he could recall being so taken by her appearance. It was as though he was seeing her for the first time, and she looked stunningly beautiful. A feeling of deep remorse passed through his body as he realized how shamelessly he had behaved all these years. She was his wife, all he really needed in facing life. And yet, he had cheated her in so many ways. Well, at that moment, he decided that was going to change. From here on, he was going to be a different person, worthy of her love. Before leaving, when he kissed her, she noticed a tenderness that had long been missing. She was affected warmly, and at the same time, a trickle of dread passed through her body like a cold shiver.

*****

The president climbed the stairs of the platform to a wild roar from the crowd. Moving to the podium, he shook hands with all the visiting dignitaries. Speaking into the mike, he thanked everyone for their presence and invitation. He then got into his prepared speech.

Bobby opened the hotel room window. Randy placed his spotting scope on the desk and zeroed in the podium where the president was beginning his speech. Randy had instructed Bobby that there would be two parts to what was now to take place: One, Bobby would place his crosshairs onto the victim, and then, two, he would wait until Randy said "now!" Randy wanted the crowd to be at the maximum noise level when the shot occurred.

Glancing at a nearby flagpole, Bobby saw the wind was at dead calm. Not a ripple on the flag. Perfect! Slowly, he raised the weapon's butt to his shoulder and found the victim's forehead; he waited for Randy's signal. Randy, knowing Bobby was ready, waited for the proper moment. The president briefly reached down to grab a drink of water, so Randy was hesitant. But when the president straightened back up, he made a comment that erupted the crowd. At that moment, Randy said "now!" The hotel room exploded with the rifle report.

Now it will never be known as to whether Bobby lowered his shot ever so slightly or whether a sudden whirlwind of air caused the rifle bullet to drop, but the bullet didn't hit the president in the head but instead tore through his sternum, ripped through his heart, and exited on his left side through his rib cage. John Bugman, the party chairman sitting to the president's left and slightly behind, was starting to rise to join the crowd's enthusiasm when the bullet, not yet spent, hit him at the side and back of his head, exploding brains and blood upon many of the dignitaries on the platform. Everybody on that stage jumped up. The scene became total chaos.

When the president was hit, he was thrown back and collapsed in a heap on the floor of the platform. Secret Service men dashed from on and off the platform and carried him to one of the motorcade limousines and rushed him off to the hospital. It was only a formality because the president was killed instantly. John Bugman's fate was equally sealed.

Back in the hotel room, Bobby knew he had hit the victim. Randy, seeing the president collapse, turned toward Bobby with a huge smile on his face. Reaching for Bobby's right arm, as though to shake it, he thrust the needle of a syringe into Bobby's needle-tracked arm. Just one more needle hole in the user's arm. Who was to know the difference? The lethal drug cocktail took hold immediately as Bobby's surprised look turned to complete submission to the drug's effect. In a matter of minutes, Bobby was no more. Randy placed the syringe in Bobby's hand, and when he let go, Bobby's arm fell loose, and the syringe fell to the floor, just as though he had dropped the syringe after using it. Quickly taking the spotting scope and placing it in his tote bag, Randy walked out the hotel room, down the stairway, and out onto the street. Walking rather than running, he engaged no suspicion, and two blocks later, he was picked up in a nondescript car. Randy was never to be seen or heard from again.

It wasn't long, and the Secret Service and the police authorities were scouring the row of hotels opposite the lakefront park. They eventually found Bobby with the rifle still on the desk. The rifle was found to be totally untraceable. Working back on Bobby's history, he was easily identified. When his apartment landlord reported him missing, they were able to put the pieces together. His obvious use of drugs and a stained military background and it was easy for them to chalk this assassination off as a drug-crazed ex-Army misfit who wanted to take revenge. They tried to find out who his pusher was, but that led to nowhere. It seemed the pusher had just recently been killed by a hit-and-run driver. After an investigation of some duration, the case was considered closed, describing the assassin as acting alone.

On the day of the assassination, Vice President Sam Butford was attending a meeting with several senators in the Senate office building when Secret Service men entered the meeting office and ushered the vice president out. Explaining the circumstances, the VP was taken to the Oval Office where the swearing in was to take place. Sam, taken completely by surprise, merely followed instructions. Things were happening so quickly he did not take in the magnitude of what seemed like surreal circumstances. By the time he went to bed that night, he went from second man to president of the United States. He had wanted the job, but he never expected it to be like this. Now, faced with a shocked nation, he was thrust into the most powerful position on earth. It was to sink in gradually during the night, then with all its glory by morning. Sam felt it was fate that put him in this position. Little did he know, the force behind the throne would soon be felt but not all together unwelcome by Sam Butford. Sam liked power, and he would soon thrive on the idea of helping The Committee and the party achieve their goals.

CHAPTER 5

The Onset of Change

The nations shock and national mourning passed with all the usual affect you would expect from such a disaster. The funeral, along with the respect and adoration the nation gave the deceased president, soon faded into another historic memory of one of those tragic events that the country never hoped to experience. And yet, just as in the past, it happened, and despite it all, the life of the people and country moved on.

The Committee, though satisfied the event took place as planned, wasn't entirely happy that the chairman of the C3P was also terminated. It meant a new chairman, and they quickly turned their attention to the proper selection. It was concluded that the chief of staff for the former president was suited for the job, and they immediately implemented the mechanics to get him elected as the new chairman of C3P. President Butford selected a new chief of staff, one who was administratively very capable but with a secret persona that would bring nothing but problems to the president and eventually release a chain of events that would affect The Committee and the C3P.

*****

The country was now entering an era where the civil rights movement was growing in intensity. The Committee was now free to implement its tenets. By initiating actions through its secret functionaries, the C3P was able to gain the sympathy and following of minorities and the underprivileged.

The Committee assembled its foursome at its mountain retreat, and Merlin conducted the meeting. He started by emphasizing that the minorities and underprivileged were a significant and growing segment of the voting population.

"By appearing to advance the cause of civil rights within the C3P, we gain the opportunity to win over their complete following. Middle- and upper-class citizens will look upon us as a caring and concerned party and will tend to lean our way. Make no mistake, we are not doing this in the best interest of the minorities or underprivileged. We are doing it for the sake of our objectives. It is a fact that when the poor and indigent are provided for, when they have little or nothing, they will obligate themselves to those who they see as their providers. By developing programs that are framed as a redistribution of wealth through taxation, the government justifies taxes for the supposed good. We can build a huge welfare system that will make funds available to our party like never before. Because of this, we create a whole new element of contribution to our cause."

Juno interjected, "It also has been long known that for us to institute true socialism, it has to be done by weakening the economic state of the country. When that happens, we are in the best position to implement more of our intents. We increasingly weaken the economic state of the nation every time we bring about laws that increase bureaucracy and strain the treasury.

"In keeping with this strategy, if planned and instituted carefully, we create a welfare system that is so fraught with entitlement to all levels of supposed need (e.g., single parents, low income, homeless, handicapped, immigrants, et cetera) that it will make great demands on the nation's economic resources. But the real issue to our benefit is that it will require a huge bureaucracy to manage it all. This is our objective: to create the bureaucracy, not the traditional notion of caring for the poor and those in need. Long term, our socialist intent is to level the playing field by eliminating the middle and upper classes, raise the lower class, and create our intended two class system: the elite (bureaucrats and politicians) and the working class (everybody else). Gentlemen and lady, the more strain we put on the Treasury, the more we serve our purpose. This is in keeping with Article XII: 'Since the bureaucrats and politicians control the use of funds, they can enrich themselves at the expense of the population and remain the elite.'"

Merlin then introduced one more element of conversation. "The civil rights movement has at this time a leader who has gained national attention. His following grows with each passing day. No one knows where it will eventually lead, but it could create a great disruption to our cause if this leader gains power and directs attention away from our party. This must not happen, and we must determine a means of controlling this outcome to our advantage."

Merlin offered a possible solution that would strengthen the movement but nullify the leader's active power. He said, "If it were possible to make him a martyr, we could memorialize him before his people and solidify this bloc of the population."

Ivan rose and began walking the floor. "How can we possibly make him a martyr? To me, this is wishful thinking. Do you realize what we would have to do to bring about such a ridiculous notion?"

Casper had no hesitation in responding, "It just so happens that we have information that there is a disgruntled and very bigoted individual who has been making bold statements among certain clandestine groups. If we work it out right, he might be the one who could make martyrdom happen."

The discussion that followed was heated and full of rancor and misgivings. But, in the end, The Committee decided to let Casper investigate the possibilities and report back.

*****

Sam Butford embraced his presidential responsibilities with vigor and enthusiasm. The C3P chairman, recently elected, was charged with maintaining the secrecy of the

Articles of Acquisition and informing the president of their existence. President Butford was not at all reticent about what the articles stood for. It was all right up his alley.

Sam's background was very different from Cecil Howard's. Sam was born on a farm out West; it was too small to be called a ranch. His parents had scoured out a living raising a few crops and some livestock and doing cooperative farmwork with the neighbors. Sam never liked the farm. Bookish at an early age through his mother's urgings, he spent a lot of time reading. Through his books, he had eyes to the world and his country. He made up his mind early that if there was a way he could make a difference in the world, he would pursue that end.

Fate plays strange tricks. Sam's parents lost their farm due to a mortgage foreclosure. Now faced with destitution, the family was forced to move into the city to find work and the hope of someone giving them a place to live. Though Sam's parents would manage to eke out a living during the remainder of their lives, Sam was old enough to know that he didn't like people or businesses having that much power over the common man. He felt that there must be a way to control lives for the better. Being the reader that he was, he began to study the philosophies of social reformers.

Sam was forced to take a job somewhere, and that somewhere happened to be with a county road maintenance crew. Having gained some knowledge on the farm in working with equipment and general carpentry, he at least had some skill. The work was not much to his liking. But the fact that he was more literate than his fellow workers gave him an edge when it came to the filling out of paperwork. His supervisors saw him as having a great deal of potential, and they moved him up into more responsible and less labor-intensive positions. It didn't take him long to discover that with each move upward in position, he gained greater opportunity to exercise control over his subordinates. Ironically, he liked that feeling.

In no time, Sam worked himself up from laborer to the head of the county road and bridge maintenance department. This position required working with contractors and the county workers. These contracts normally were subject to bidding, lowest bidder getting the job. However, Sam had the discretionary authority to throw bids out based on his judgment. This he did whenever he didn't like a particular contractor. Then the day came when a position in politics was in the offering if he steered work toward an influence peddler's preferred company. Through this device, Sam entered political life. Running first as county commissioner, the political machine of that county backed him, and he won. Later, he decided to run for a US Senate seat. With the party fully behind him and the constituents convincingly motivated by the party, Sam became US Senator. Firmly in a high political office, his dream of a place to make a difference, and the ability to influence the lives of people, he attained the objective he had aspired to. It was now that his ideologies fully kicked in. He felt that the government must be the caretaker of the people, and he, as part of an elite, must be one of the planners that would make that happen.

*****

The Far East conflict that the country was involved in as advisors now grew into a war of attrition. Micromanaging the military in the application of policy turned the whole thing into a political and military morass. Objectives on the ground were dictated by Washington, and more troops and matériel were required day by day. Casualties rose, and the American population got increasingly discontented with the US involvement. The discontent grew and spilled over into the colleges and universities. Draft dodging became commonplace. The whole business was a growing danger to the C3P. The administration was being drawn further and further into a monster of their own making.

On the positive side for the C3P, due to unfortunate circumstances, it seemed a prominent leader of the civil rights movement had been assassinated by a lone gunman. The gunman got away, but an investigation seemed to indicate they had significant leads as to who the gunman was. Nevertheless, a martyr to the civil rights movement came into being, and C3P played it to every advantage.

During Sam Butford's term of office, some of the most sweeping changes in the civil rights movement and general entitlements came about. Despite the evil intent of the C3P in its motives to support the less prosperous of the nation, there was much good that rose to the surface in providing for the less fortunate. It was an irony, but they always said: "That out of every great evil inevitably comes a greater good."

The C3P was reaping a big harvest in winning more and more of the lower class to the party. The combination of a growing war and ever larger cash demands to meet new entitlements put great pressure on the Treasury. Deficits grew. To The Committee, almost everything was going as planned as far as ideological objectives to weaken the economy. However, the general population was starting to lose confidence in President Butford and the C3P for many reasons. The civil rights movement was erupting as a series of conflagrations around the country. The Far East conflict, unbridled rioting at universities, city ghettos burned and looted—all were unsettling the nation, and the administration didn't seem to have solutions for these problems. Russia was growing in nuclear and military strength, exerting pressure around the world. All added to the president's woes. President Butford, faced with increasing crises of one kind or another, grew weary of the pressure and frustration of office. Though he was encouraged by his party to run for office for the next term, he decided he would not, much to the chagrin of the C3P.

The Committee, hearing of the president's intentions, knew it would be difficult to win an election against the American Traditional Party (ATP), considering all the negativity toward the administration and congress. But there was another reason it looked difficult. The president's chief of staff was caught in scandalous circumstances. It seemed he was a sex deviate who liked to expose himself. He did it in one of the government washrooms and was caught in the act by security police. The president was so embarrassed by this that he called in the head of the FBI and established an enhanced system of background checks and security clearance for all White House office and administrative personnel. Staffed by an FBI investigator, this process would be a permanent method to clear personnel for any position within the White House or its related administrative adjuncts for administrations to come. Once and for all, maybe the president could be protected from such scandal. The action was well-received, but it was too late for this administration. The damage was done, and it would contribute to the party's loss at the next election.

The FBI chose a candidate to head up the background checks of White House personnel hires. He was a young rising star in the department named Jim Cooper. Born of modest parents, Jim worked his way through college by working on road construction as a general laborer. For extra money during school, he enrolled in ROTC and picked up some grant-in-aid money through volunteer programs and school side jobs. Graduating with a degree in history, he entered active duty with the Army as an army intelligence officer with the rank of second lieutenant. He did well on his four years of active duty and rose to the rank of captain. Married to his college sweetheart, they had two children. Jim applied with the FBI upon separation from active duty and was readily accepted. His top-secret clearances made it that much easier. Soon he was involved in crucial FBI work. Jim thrived on this activity and rose rapidly in recognition within the department. So, when the White House job came up, he was one of the first to be considered. After an interview process that included the president, Jim was chosen. Fate was to play a historic role in his occupation of this position.

*****

As an outgrowth of the civil rights movement, the feminist movement became increasingly prevalent. Women's groups around the nation began to rise up in hopes of strengthening women's rights. The C3P, seeing the opportunity to exploit this movement, took the position of supporting this effort and used every means to strengthen the cause for their own gain. By doing so, they endeared themselves to the movement and, in keeping with their creed, exploited the movement. Planned parenthood and abortion topics were promoted on an ever larger scale, and laws were introduced to push for abortion as a woman's right. Every liberal segment of the population was tapped to support all the issues concerning women's rights. Housewives were demeaned as nonproductive slaves to a vocation of indenture. The media, motion picture industry, and a growing pop culture diluted marriage as an institution. The C3P received major support from this growing liberal segment of society. With the media, movies, and pop culture propagandizing women's rights issues, they seemed to think important; the legitimate improvements necessary in women's rights were subverted by the excess demands the C3P and their constituency wished to employ. Along with some of the positive things that the movement granted in women's opportunities, much was directed toward abortion, planned parenthood, and sexual freedom.

Once this feminist movement got a foothold, it influenced traditional family settings. Feminists so influenced American women that a reformation in the family began to take place. Here's a perfect example:

Jane Jefferson was a college graduate who met her husband in college. Her degree was in accounting and business management. The two of them married soon after college, and Jane became pregnant with their first child. Not wanting to go to work right away, she spent her time at home raising their baby. She had no complaints, and her husband had a good job. In another year, they had a second child, and their life, though a struggle not uncommon with young families, was a happy one. Jane had old friends from college who had entered the business world and were now acquiring some new feminist attitudes about what a woman's vocation should be. Certainly, the idea of being at home did not fit their idea of what a woman should be doing, and they began to put pressure on Jane about her submission to a housewife's perceived service of indenture while her husband could enjoy pursuing his career. Jane began to have second thoughts about her life. Even though it was pleasant and fulfilling, she started feeling she was cheating herself in what she had prepared herself educationally and then not carrying it through at this time of her life. Enforcing this feeling was all the media, TV entertainment, and motion picture infusion of feminist derision of traditional culture.

Jane talked to her husband and told him she was now going to find a job. It would help the family finances and give her the opportunity to pursue a career she originally intended. He had no problem with it because he too was listening to the current feminist propaganda and started feeling guilty about presumably holding back his wife.

It didn't take too long for Jane to find a job with a marketing firm as an administrative specialist. She quickly worked her way up and found herself in an important marketing specialist position. She was to travel regularly and would make presentations to the client base.

Jane's job required that the family find a childcare center for the children. This added cost to the family budget, but it seemed worth it. One car was no longer adequate because her husband needed his, and she would be working different hours or occasionally traveling. Insurance and fuel cost became an additional consideration. Jane couldn't go to work in just any clothes, so she had to buy and maintain a new wardrobe. It wasn't long, and family household expenses grew to a whole new level, and to start with, everything Jane brought in financially went out to pay her new bills. Credit cards seldom used before were now a necessity to cover shortfalls in between. Too tired to make meals at home after work, restaurants became a too frequent choice for supper when noon meals had already added financial cost to Jane's decision to pursue her career. A side problem cropped up now that the kids were in childcare. They were coming home with more illnesses, and doctor bills, relatively nonexistent before, became a regular occurrence. It seemed the illnesses had more strains with new side effects that didn't always get eased by traditional home remedies or aspirin.

The most insidious and perhaps devastating effect on the family was the increased pressure on Jane and her husband. Her husband coming home in the evening before Jane started working found a nice meal and a wife eager to sit and talk with him as they commiserated their daily activities. There was affection and an appreciation of each other. The children were happy and psychologically and physically healthy. Now neither Jane nor her husband wanted to talk about anything, least of all work. Tired, they were sometimes short with the kids, and meals were thrown together or they went out to eat. Also, Jane started finding that the people she was working with had an independent quality about them. They were more into themselves than any obligation to others. Though she found this to be repulsive at the start, she gradually began to acquire the same quality herself as she prospered within the company. At the same time, her husband started to become more distant to her, and she started to resent it. Her husband, now coming home to chaos and frustration over meals, kids, and a careered wife, found himself wanting companionship that seemingly he no longer had.

This scenario played out around the country among a great number of families, not just with educated family members but with all levels of married couples as the feminist movement grew. Young children were greatly affected as families broke up or the children became latchkey. Divorces grew at an unprecedented rate, and families, as the center of society, began to come apart.

One of the side effects of all this was the ever-increasing growth of the state departments of children and family. The government sized this department to meet the challenge of an ever-growing number of dysfunctional families. The C3P benefited again as bigger government was applied to the situation. And the C3P played the sympathy card hard and strong. Protecting the children was natural to the population, as it should be, but C3P was only looking for what they could gain politically. Who would oppose them?

*****

As Sam Butford pondered his term of office, in retrospect, he considered it a great accomplishment for his party. He was right because during his term, new entitlement programs for welfare were implemented on a massive scale. The civil rights movement came into its own with all of its benefits and its complications that a society didn't easily adjust to. The feminist movement changed the way women viewed themselves. Minority groups now started looking for new ways to influence the majority cultures. The terms *bias*, *bigotry*, *prejudice,* and *homophobia* became part of a jargon that debased anything or anybody that would even think negative thoughts about overreactions to the issue of equal rights. Minorities became just as bigoted as their opposites, except they were allowed to get away with it. Soon those persons who would even discuss the issue of the minority cultures that didn't want to work, single women with children from one or more fathers, those who never married or were working the welfare system instead of finding jobs, were considered bigoted, biased, or without compassion. The C3P played a big role in belittling the American Traditional Party for doing just that. Even the discussion of how to deal with ghetto communities and their social culture brought derision against the ATP by the C3P. The C3P was gaining momentum with every new increase in the welfare system.

President Sam Butford, sitting in the Oval Office, reminiscing over his term with his chief of staff and the party chairman, casually allowed it to slip that "The Committee should be very happy with the progress that the C3P has made during my time in office."

What Sam didn't know was that an aide called to the Oval Office overheard the comment as he entered the room. The aide, leaving the Oval Office, bumped into background investigator Jim Cooper.

"Jim, do you know of a committee that the president refers to in conjunction with the C3P?"

Jim responded, "Well, I suppose it's the C3P committee that plans for the party and all its fundraising and political agendas."

"No, it doesn't sound that way to me. It sounds more like a special group."

"Well, if it is, I can't imagine what it could be." Jim responded with an inquisitive look on his face.

Although Jim gave the comments little recognition, it raised big questions in his mind. In his background checks of various personnel getting clearance to work in the White House, there were suggestions of something going on about the people directed to work at the White House. There were curious patterns. He couldn't put his finger on them then, but now he thought there might be something to all this.

Jim Cooper was a dedicated and serious believer in the precepts of the Constitution and had great respect for how this nation was founded and what it offered to the citizens. When he started working in his new capacity and his exposure to the people working in the White House during President Sam Butford's term, he noticed that there was a direction coming from what seemed to be outside the C3P as he knew it. This gnawed at him. Now it seemed that it was becoming more obvious, particularly since the White House aide verbalized it as well. He decided he would be more alert to these new symptoms. One thing was for sure: Although he was charged with doing background checks for clearance for all new White House hires and appointments, he had no authority to accept or reject anyone. All he could do was make recommendations. The final decision was up to the president and/or his appointed representative. In Jim's mind, there were several questionable approvals.

The final days of President Sam Butford's term were at hand. The American Traditional Party had won the election as everybody suspected it would. The new president-elect whom years before, while running against Cecil Howard, had lost principally because of Cecil Howard's ability to connect with the voting public. Now the new ATP president had been elected because the population was looking for change. The Far East war had been badly managed and had lost its favor completely with America. Civil unrest continued to plague many cities as the civil rights movement took hold. The new president won on his identity, and he had campaigned heavily to bring change people thought the country needed. His statesmanship was creditable, and foreign relations were badly needed. Despite all these positive traits, not everyone felt he was the best alternative. He lacked the one thing the American Traditional Party never seemed to be able to acquire in a candidate: an ability to connect verbally with the people. Missing was that certain charisma that good leaders need to win the affection and trust of the people. Notwithstanding deficits in his personality, the new president, to his credit, applied himself with dedication and vigor. Definitely conservative in his character, he still commanded respect by his reputation.

While the Sam Butford's administration was transitioning out of office during the days before the inauguration of the incoming president, Jim Cooper accidentally uncovered an unexpected bit of information that made his blood run cold. Never expecting to discover active political figures involved in actions blatantly detrimental to his country, it shook him up and raised his ire as never before. Members of the C3P, now leaving jobs they had for these many years, were violently upset over their party's loss. Unguarded statements were made to one another, always believing they were among their own. Jim Cooper, having been around for a while, was sometimes overlooked for what he really was, and Jim would hear some of these comments.

One day, while making his rounds, Jim Cooper ran into one of the C3P loyalists who was visibly angry over the transition to the new administration. Noticing his frustration, Jim asked him, "What's up?"

"Damn it, Jim, I don't know where your political feelings lay, but I can't get it out of my mind as how we are supposed to implement the C3P strategy when we're working against the ATP and are not privy to what the complete strategy of the C3P is! It seems only a few key people know what it is. And would you believe it? It's locked up in a damn safe in the party's national office. Can you imagine? It's so dadgum secret that it has to be kept in a safe. At least, I think that's where it is. The party chairman is the only one who has access to it and reveals it to only a few people, and I assume our president—now ex-president."

"You honestly believe there is a secret agenda that your party is following?"

"Yes, and it pisses me off! I am not happy with that kind of activity. I intend to get to the bottom of this cloak-and-dagger stuff somehow. And you know what else? I think there is a force behind the party moving us in their direction. I overheard the C3P chairman refer to The Committee and to articles of some kind. It's as though the party has some mysterious code of conduct that they are trying to implement, and only a few people know about it."

Jim had one more piece of this mystery and was hopeful he could "wheedle" more information out of this individual. That was not to be because this person suddenly disappeared; he apparently asked too many questions. When asking others where he went, they would only respond that he left to go back to his former career, and no one was clear as to where that might be.

Soon Inauguration Day came and went, and Jim Cooper was continuing to clear new candidates for work at the White House. He still was haunted by the things he learned in the previous administration and was determined to find out what it all meant. Kept busy with his current responsibilities, it gave him little time to do any private investigating. But that wouldn't stop him from keeping his eyes open.

CHAPTER 6

Propaganda

The Committee met after Inauguration Day in their mountain retreat to review the overall situation. They had lost the election, but during the past administration, many of their objectives were met. The Supreme Court was about to settle the issue of women's rights when it came to abortion, giving an almost carte blanche approval to allowing women to choose if and when to abort their child for whatever reason. Abortion would now be used as part of the C3P platform. Things were moving well for the C3P and The Committee felt it was time to turn up the heat on exploiting the liberal establishment.

> Propaganda...for the most part must
> be aimed at emotions and only to a very
> limited degree at the so-called intellect.
> All propaganda must be popular, and its
> intellectual level must be adjusted to the

most limited intelligence among those it is addressed to. Consequently, the greater the mass it is intended to reach, the lower its purely intellectual level will have to be.

The receptivity of the great masses is very limited, their intelligence is small, but their power of forgetting is enormous. In consequence, all effective propaganda must be limited to a very few points and must harp on these in slogans until the last member of the public understands what you want him to understand by your slogan. (Adolf Hitler, *Mein Kampf*)

"We all know the power of Adolf Hitler's propaganda machine in convincing his countrymen to rally to National Socialism."

Merlin put it into perspective.

"The liberal establishment is our key to getting the general population to abandon traditional moral concepts. As article 4 of our charter demands, we must degrade traditional moral concepts to pave the way for socialist involvement through government intervention. By using the media and the entertainment industry and employing the use of freedom of speech, we can get these industries to distort the truth and allow the implementation of a free-living and free-thinking society with minimized moral conscience and an obligation only to civil authority. This means also that liberal business owner and senior executive officers will push the envelope in acquiring personal wealth to the detriment of their own business and/or their clients. This will impact the general welfare of the economy so as to require more government intervention.

"As the general public takes on a more liberal and less traditional moral lifestyle, families will continue to break up. Though this will add strife to the population, they will look to the government to help fill their needs. As this need increases, so will there be the need for bigger government to fix it, and we will use every propaganda means necessary to accomplish this."

Ivan interjected, "So what you are saying is that by employing slogans and themes, we will be able to drum-beat ideas into the public so that they take up our causes as theirs and therefore cement our hold on their thinking."

"Exactly!" said Merlin. "Here are some examples: women's rights, change, homophobia, unfair, pro-choice, equal opportunity, eco-friendly, 'it's the economy,' affirmative action, civil rights, civil liberty, the religious right, the radical right, progressive, living wage, etc."

At this point, Juno added, "As we exploit liberality in business, we will find new sources of revenue to our cause. Through our selected politicians in key places, they will seek out these businesses and collude with their involvement in providing funds to preferred candidates for office. This has been done in the past, but we will be looking for unprecedented means of accomplishing this."

At this statement, Ivan asked, "How do you see this being accomplished?"

She responded, "One of these unprecedented means is through the promotion of an expansion of simplifying the ability of anyone to acquire mortgages for the purchase of homes. We need to exploit the American Dream of owning a home. We need to establish a super mortgage entity or entities to ease the conditions upon which mortgages will be approved, with the mortgage entities backed by the government. To start with, it should be a government entity. Once established, it should become a stock-traded company, with government a part owner and the public owning the rest. It needs to be done like this to subtle the public and the ATP into believing it's the right approach.

"Then we move *our* people in to run the major aspects of these entities. Now legally able to hire political action committees to encourage our ideas in Congress, we'll increase the volume of activity to constitute trillions of dollars in mortgages. We will be able to skim off these ventures millions for the C3P through contributions and independent pro-party, political activist groups. We will enrich our people involved in these entities and then watch as the system exploits the population. By offering mortgages with eased mechanisms, the mortgage industry will be rife with fraud and corruption at every level. The mortgage industry will eventually implode, effectively affecting almost every aspect of the economy, and government will have no recourse but to intervene in unprecedented bailouts of several industries regardless of which president is in office. We will have implemented the first stages of serious government nationalization of banks, financial institutions, and industry."

Merlin interjected, "How do we get industry nationalized as part of this process?"

"Easy! As we encourage and integrate liberal chief executives into the high places in industry, they will seek to plunder the assets of their corporations through unrealistic reward packages. Coupled with a close association with the unions, they will ignore the consumer, appease the laborers, and pay for their extravagance off the buying public. That too will cause an implosion of some of the biggest union-controlled companies in America, particularly the auto industry, and eventually an economic catastrophe within their ranks that only the government can seemingly resolve. That's when it will be easy to nationalize."

Yes, it seemed The Committee was well on the way to shaking up the country. After further discussion on many matters, The Committee meeting broke up with their agenda well in hand.

CHAPTER 7

A Safe Bet

Thomas Wilford Sullivan, the American Traditional Party president, was settling into his job as the leader of the country, and his administration faced very challenging tasks. The Far East conflict was a mess, and the only solution was an exit strategy. Civil rights problems were continuing around the country although there were some signs of calm entering into the picture. Sadly, soldiers coming back from the Far East were being treated poorly by some of the population, a grave injustice toward them since the conflict was not of their making and they were just doing their duty. Russia was still building their nuclear arsenal, and the concept of mutual destruction was being talked about at The Pentagon.

By his second term, President Sullivan had put the Far East problem behind the country's concerns by pulling out of a war that had been badly run and had carried on too long for all the wrong reasons but not without embarrassment to a country that was used to winning its battles.

Economic issues, Russia, and dealing with C3P in its increasing political influence over the population were continuing challenges. However, his biggest challenge was about to face him.

Jim Cooper, freed briefly from his daily FBI duties, decided to ride over to the office building where the C3P had its headquarters. Curious to see what activity was taking place there, he ambled by the office and took note of where it was, what floor of the building, and what apparent traffic went in and out. Nothing seemed out of the ordinary other than the office was entered into from a door exposed only to the hallway, no window sections to see into the office, and only a relatively obscure sign mentioning the offices of the C3P headquarters. The number of people going in and out was not unusual although all of them seemed to be very serious in their appearance and demeanor. There didn't seem to be any kind of cordiality among any of them. He even tried to exchange pleasantries, receiving only half-hearted replies or silence.

Jim decided he needed to be invited into that office somehow. He didn't know how, but he had an idea on how he could work it out. He'd use his background checking as an excuse to see someone at the C3P office. He opined that he just needed to find the right person to give him the proper excuse to call on the C3P headquarters. And then, out of the blue, walking toward him, grinning from ear to ear, was an old acquaintance from the C3P's previous administration. George Pendergast had been an aide in the

White House, and Jim Cooper and he had, on many occasions, conversed with each other. After exchanging pleasantries, George wondered what Jim was doing in this office building. Jim, of course, said he had some official dealings in the area.

"You know, George? I have never been inside the C3P's national headquarters office. I'm curious to see what goes on in there."

"Sure, Jim, let's go in. I've got to see the C3P chair, so I'll give you the full treatment."

Entering the office, Jim again noticed that everyone was moving and acting in sort of an emotionless state. Maybe it was the loss of the election that had them in such a funk, but it just wasn't his kind of atmosphere. George walked up to the C3P chairman's secretary and said he was there for an appointment, and she ushered him right in. George grabbed Jim, and the two went into the chairman's office.

Walking into the office, Jim noticed that this was a very messy guy. A coffee table in the center of the room was littered with old used paper coffee cups. Newspapers were strewn here and there as if read and then discarded into the corner of a couch or on an end table. File folders were stacked in loose fashion, some opened, some closed, and the whole office gave the appearance of disorganization. As they approached the chairman's desk, he looked up and, seeing Jim Cooper with George, said, "What's he doing here? Who is he?"

George, caught off guard, replied, "Hey, take it easy. This is an old friend. He's with the FBI, and I just brought him in to see your operation. He's never been here before, so I didn't think it would be a big deal to let him have a look. He just happened to be in the building when we bumped into each other."

The chairman's expression changed, and putting on a forced appearance of cordiality, he said, "Oh, I'm sorry, I was in the middle of things, and I was not prepared for an impromptu meeting. Forgive me if you thought me rude."

Jim assured him it was okay. And then he noticed that on the chairman's desk was a plaque that read: "Article 1: The end will justify the means." The chairman, noticing that Jim Cooper saw the plaque said, "I see you noticed the plaque on my desk. Yes, that's part of our emphasis to get things done. What we are really saying is we must be pro-active in all that we do to maintain our party platform. It's a reminder to all of us in the C3P of what we are all about in creating a progressive and greater America."

Jim listened but didn't like the sound of it. He accepted the chairman's response in a casual manner, and the chairman seemed relieved that he could move on to another subject. Also, Jim did notice a safe behind the chairman's desk. Could this be the safe that was alluded to in his talks with previous party members who were frustrated with the secrecy surrounding the C3P's actions? It must be!

After a few moments, Jim said he had to be on his way, and George escorted him out into the hallway, and they bid each other a cordial farewell.

As Jim walked away, he reflected on the plaque on the chairman's desk. If it had said "The end will justify the means," it might have not been as obvious to him, but by the fact that it was preceded by "Article 1" meant that the people he had been talking to, who brought up this articles thing, really weren't imagining it. In fact, the idea that there were articles, plural, meant that there was the possibility of an assemblage of various subjects in some kind of list or proclamation that was being used as a blueprint for implementation of some form or another. He mused, *"The end will justify the means" by itself is a nefarious statement.* It was anybody's guess at what the other articles might be. Unfortunately, the only way to really know would be to get into that safe. Therein lay the real problem.

Jim decided it was time to talk to his immediate supervisor. There was definitely something going on, and he needed to share his concerns.

Jack Watkins was a straight shooter. A career FBI man, he grew through the ranks and was wise in the ways of the department and politics. As Jim Cooper's supervisor, he was the one man who could steer Jim right if he felt Jim was getting off course. So Jim set up a meeting with Jack.

When Jim Cooper walked into Jack Watkins's office, Jack was sitting at his desk with his ever-present pipe firmly set between his teeth. Looking up at Jim, he exclaimed, "Why, Jim? Why such a morose look on your face? You would think that you had the world on your shoulders. Is this meeting going to be as serious as all that?"

"Jack, I believe there is something going on in the C3P that is not exactly what I believe a free democratic nation should be about. The signs are everywhere, but the whole picture is still ambiguous and vague."

"What do you mean?" Jack's face turned serious.

"I mean that there seems to be present a force and a plan that could be against our democratic principles yet using our democratic process to defile the original intentions of the forefathers of this country."

Jack, setting his pipe down, took a more animated interest in what Jim was saying. "Can you be more specific?"

Jim, seeing that he now had Jack's fullest attention, said, "Well, have you heard the term 'articles' bandied about in your movements through Washington?"

Upon hearing the word *articles*, Jack stood up and said, "Now it's funny that you should bring that up. In some of the miscellaneous investigative work that we are currently involved in, 'articles' was referred to. I'm not at liberty to say how or what work it relates to, but it did seem to bear interest because it was so inexplicable when used."

By now, Jack took Jim's concern seriously because he knew that Jim always had his feet squarely on the ground and was not likely to go off half-cocked. So he asked Jim what he thought should be done.

"How do you want to proceed on this?"

"Well, I thought it should be taken up with the president."

Surprised at this response, Jack, looking at Jim, intently said, "You really think it's that serious?"

"Yes, I do, and with your permission, I have the ability to approach him since I'm involved with him regularly on clearance matters."

Jack paced the floor a bit and then said, "You realize that I will have to advise the assistant director about this."

"Yes, I understand, but I think you should advise him *after* I approach the president. If you advise him beforehand, he might not let it happen, and I believe it would jeopardize any ability to find out what this is all about."

Jack looked leery, but with a condescending sigh, he okayed Jim's approach, saying, "You know, of course, that you are asking me to stick my neck out for you?"

"Yes, I know. But if you feel as I do, we should proceed to get this figured out. If you don't feel as I do, as your subordinate, you can shut me down right now."

Jack didn't like being pushed into a corner, but this "articles" thing seemed to take on a new light.

"Okay! But I want to know what the president says when you approach him. If this goes south, you and I will both be on the hot seat."

*****

The president was sitting in the Oval Office when his secretary came in.

"Mr. President, Agent Jim Cooper requests a meeting with you as soon as it is convenient."

"Who?"

"Jim Cooper, the FBI staff member who handles staff clearance investigations."

"Oh yes, Jim, good man, I like him. We need more good people like him around. By all means. When does he want to meet?"

"As soon as you are willing. He's very anxious to get with you."

70

"Very well, have him come in now, if he's ready."

"Yes, Mr. President, he's waiting outside. I'll show him in."

Jim Cooper entered the Oval Office to find the president in what appeared to be a jovial mood.

"Good morning, Mr. President."

"Good morning, Jim, take a seat and tell me what's on your mind."

"Well, Mr. President, it's not easy to bring up what I'm about to say. You might think me a fool or you might think me an alarmist. In any case, I wouldn't be here before you now if I didn't think that there was something going on. I believe it's having and will continue to have national consequences."

"Good grief, man! What are you talking about?"

"Well, sir, it is my belief that there is a plan to change the landscape of government in this country to the detriment of our forefather's original intentions. I believe this effort has been initiated by the C3P. I believe the plan is in the safe of the national headquarters office. And I believe somehow we must learn the entire plan."

The president shifted uncomfortably in his chair. Knowing Jim was a man with no screwy agendas, he asked him, "Tell me why you believe this."

"Well, I'll start by asking you if you have heard the term "articles" used in your travels among your political or nonpolitical contacts."

The president sat up erect in his chair. During the transition to his administration, one of his staff members found a crumpled piece of paper with article 1 to article

71

13 scrawled on it in the ex-president's hand. No follow-up description of each article was written on the paper. At the time, the president gave little notice but thought it odd. Now here was Jim bringing up articles once again.

"Yes, Jim, as a matter of fact, I have. It's not so much that I have heard it but the fact that I saw 'articles' written by my predecessor, 1 to 13 and no description."

"Mr. President, without realizing it, you just added a new dimension to this. You indicate that there are thirteen articles. That's the first assurance that there are several. I actually saw article 1 on the C3P chairman's desk, at least, the beginnings of it, and it read: 'The end will justify the means.' I think you can see now why I believe there is more going on than meets the eye."

"Jim, it looks like you may have uncovered something that bears looking into."

The president turned, looked out the window, and sat silent for a few moments. Then, with a quick turn and looking straight at Jim, he said, "I don't want you to become involved in any actual activity to acquire these so-called articles because I want you to have the independent freedom of movement and separation to acquire information. I will assemble some of my closest cabinet or administrative confidants to determine a course of action. Should you have occasion to discover any new information, please let me know. In the meantime, when it's appropriate, I'll be in touch with you."

"Thank you, Mr. President. I am at your disposal."

With that, Jim left the president's office, and now he had to report to his boss. Jim immediately went to Jack

AN AGE OF TREASON

Watkins's office filled Jack in on all that the president had to say.

"So the president *has* had exposure to the subject of articles. This is beginning to take on interesting possibilities. If the president is interested enough to look into this with his confidants, then it must have merit. I'll brief the assistant director. I'm not sure what his take will be on any of this. Keep me informed on any further developments and thank you for getting back to me."

Jim Cooper could only guess at what might happen next.

Jack Watkins met with the assistant director of the FBI. The AD was trying to posture himself to become the new director because the present director was retiring shortly, and the president was to make a replacement announcement at any time. This was on Jack's mind, and he wasn't sure how this new information was going to play in the AD's present frame of mind. Entering the assistant director's office, the AD said, "Come in, Jack. What have you got going?"

"I'm afraid it is still a bit of a mystery, but I want to bring you up to date on something that has been brought to my attention."

"Oh? If it's new to you, why am I hearing it second? It's supposed to be the other way around."

"You are right, sir. However, due to the nature of it, we thought we should take it to the president first and see if he saw merit in it."

"What in the hell did you think you were doing in taking it directly to the president without my consent first? And what do you mean when you say 'we'?"

"Well, ah, yes, sir, Jim Cooper came upon this, and since he has almost immediate contact with the president, he and I agreed that he would approach him first before coming to you. After all, you would have to get an appointment with the president, and Jim Cooper sees him on a regular basis. Our intent was not to go around you but to confirm whether the president had been exposed to similar information."

"Watkins, I'm not happy as how you went about this without my knowledge. What's done is done. And now you better tell me what's going on, and it better be damned good and as serious as you seem to think it is."

Jack filled the AD in on all that transpired. Afterward, the AD simply sank back in his chair and said, "Let me know if the president intends to act without the involvement of the FBI. If we are not a part of it, we should at least know what's going on."

Jack left the AD's office, not sure what the assistant director was thinking.

CHAPTER 8

A Bit of Larceny

The president called a meeting of his closest confidants in government. Among them were the CIA director, his national security advisor, his chief of staff, and his foreign relations advisor. One evening, all assembled in the Oval Office where the president outlined the basis for the meeting. Since all were known members of the ATP, this could be seen as a meeting of peers, looking into the intentions of the C3P and the supposed force behind the C3P.

The president led into the meeting. "Gentlemen, it has been brought to my attention that there is an agenda being played out by the C3P that is going to have serious implications in the future landscape of this country. It sounds like a series of platitudes aimed at changing how this country works and what could possibly be a basis for treason if implemented to the fullest."

The CIA director asked the president, "Are you saying that the C3P has contrived a conspiracy of sorts to undermine the democratic process?"

"No, I'm saying I suspect they will use the democratic process to strip the nation of traditions and values originated by our forefathers to accomplish or create a new order."

The national security advisor asked, "How have you come about this information? What you are presenting is of highly serious consequence, and we would never be able to go public with this without knowing there is credibility to what you are suggesting."

"You are absolutely right! We need creditable proof of their intentions. That proof is locked up in a safe in the C3P national headquarters office. The trick is how to get it. Gentlemen, I am asking you for your thoughts on how we can get that information, and I am willing to put myself at risk if this is as serious as I think it is!"

"Mr. President, do you realize what you are saying? You are willing to enter into an illegal act to satisfy your curiosity as what the C3P is supposedly planning and you are willing to risk your position as head of this country?"

"Yes, that's exactly what I am saying. If this was just political maneuvering, that would be one thing. But this is more than political. This is turning over a process this country was created under, and if it is what I think it is, it must be stopped."

"Mr. President, I think you ought to give us a more compelling reason for us to take such drastic action. It seems you are driving to a conclusion that only you seem to be convinced about. What other evidence do you have to warrant such a conclusion?"

"All right! I have been waiting to put some pieces together to determine what and when action should be taken!

"This all started when I ran against Cecil Howard the first time I attempted to get elected to the office as president. Several months after, Cecil Howard was inaugurated as the president. I had the occasion to meet with him pertaining to some foreign affairs issues I was previously involved in. At that meeting, I took the opportunity to congratulate him on his victory in the election and wished him luck in dealing with the responsibilities of our mighty nation. It was at that time that he made a statement to me. I'll never forget the look on his face as President Howard said, 'I am entering into an era within my party where the party is no longer the determiner of political action. Instead, there is a force behind the party, greater than the sum of all its parts that is establishing policy. I have not yet come to terms with this new agenda, but in a way, it is frightening. The creed that they have established is, for all intents and purposes, radical. I tell you this in strict confidence, but you need to know that there are changes coming.'

"After that, I never had the chance to meet up with him again, and as you all know, anything he did know went to the grave with him. Since then, I have seen evidence of changes in the C3P's actions that confirm what Cecil Howard alluded to. So you see, gentlemen, I feel we must act."

"Act? Act how? What do you propose?"

"That's why you all are here. The answers are in that safe at the C3P national headquarters office. We need to find a way to get to that safe, crack it, and find out what these articles are since they are the answers to what is going on. Once proven, we can take specific action to counter whatever it is they are trying to achieve."

At this point, the national security advisor said, "If we are all in agreement as to the importance of getting into that safe, if the safe is not too difficult, it's easy enough to find a yegg to open it. The trick is getting into the office and staying long enough to get what we want. We'll either need a diversion to evacuate the building or we will need to disable security systems and find a covert way to enter the office and get to the safe."

After much discussion, they all agreed the matter was serious enough to warrant drastic action. They decided that the best way would be to create a diversion, perhaps a fire evacuation by the use of a smoke device, integrate operatives with the fireman units as they entered the building, and penetrate the office as part of the routine search for sources of the fire. Plans would be established to work out details and to set a date.

The president's group put together their plan. They acquired five men, each with his own specialty and dedicated to helping the coup of getting the articles. One man could break into most safes if given sufficient time, one was good at acquiring the equipment to simulate firemen in action, one was able to acquire an appropriate vehicle, one had knowledge in using smoke bombs and their placement for maximum effect, and the last had strong arm capability should it be needed. They picked a date and set about their exploit.

Managing to get their smoke bombs into the main air-conditioning duct system for the applicable floor, smoke filled the entire floor level of the C3P national headquarters. Pandemonium broke out as the fire alarms were set off, and people started making for the exits.

The fire department was automatically alerted, and they were on the scene in minutes. As the firemen rushed into the building, the covert group infiltrated easily among the firemen, as they swiftly ascended to the office level that seemed most affected. As the firemen went from office to office searching for the fire, it allowed the invaders to go directly to the C3P national headquarters office.

Rushing in, they found the office empty, and though filled with smoke, they managed to get to the safe. When the yegg kneeled down to work the combination of the safe, he found, much to his surprise, that the safe was closed but not locked. As luck would have it, the chairman must have opened the safe, working with something from it, when the alarm went off. With smoke billowing into the office, without thinking, his first thought must have been to get his people and himself out of the building, leaving the safe unlocked.

The yegg's responsibility was to find the articles, make a copy, replace the original, and get out with a copy as soon as possible. This he did, making sure everything in the safe was as he found it. He then rushed out of the C3P headquarters and into the street, blending in with the mix of firemen and people crowded outside of the building. The other operatives were not so lucky. No sooner had the yegg left, a group of firemen, security police, and the C3P chairman entered the office.

When the alarm sounded, the party chairman was working on some political matters and had occasion to open his safe when the office suddenly filled with smoke. Turning from his work, he immediately instructed everyone to get out of the office and onto the street. Choking and hacking from the effects of acrid smoke and struggling for breath, he charged out with the rest to get to the fresh air as soon as possible. Once on the street, he realized he had left the safe unlocked. He immediately attempted to get back into the building. Undaunted, with help of a security officer, he convinced the officials to send some firemen with him so he could quickly get back to his office for a very important matter. Besides, the fire officials seemed to think there was no conflagration. A problem in the air conditioning system, probably overheated motors, was undoubtedly the cause of all the smoke. It was being investigated.

Upon entering the C3P office, the chairman wondered why the firemen they found there were particularly interested in his office. The firemen accompanying the chairman immediately noticed that these firemen were not of their fire company. And their equipment didn't match theirs either. Hearing this, the C3P chairman told the security officer to arrest the firemen in question for further interrogation. Calling backup, the security officer drew his weapon and escorted the firemen operatives out onto the street where they were placed in waiting vehicles and transported to police headquarters for booking.

In the meantime, the C3P chairman went to the safe to see if it was entered. Everything looked to be as he originally left it, and nothing was missing. The chairman, now relieved with everything seemingly intact, wondered as to why this suspicious activity took place in his office. Perhaps, it would come out after the police finished their interrogation of the suspects.

The yegg, after leaving the office building, shed his fire equipment and was picked up by his contact. Handing over the articles, the contact drove him to a drop-off point, and they parted. The contact was to give the articles to the CIA director, and he did so at a local mall. After which, the director went straight to the White House to confer with the president.

The local newspapers were having a run-of-the-mill day on siphoning and sorting the news when the phone call came, announcing the apparent smoke incident at the downtown office building housing the C3P national headquarters. In a mad scurry, the journalists took off to cover the story. Upon arriving, they came upon the scene of the firemen who were arrested. They were being loaded into a waiting vehicle. Inquiring what was going on, the journalists were told that the incident had suspicious overtones. These guys seemed to be suspects of something, and they were being taken in for further questioning. Undoubtedly, there would be follow-up stories from such a curious event, and the newspapers put their noses to the ground.

CHAPTER 9

What Now?

As the CIA director entered the Oval Office, he saw the president was in an agitated state.

"We got the articles! Mr. President, we won the battle, but I am afraid we may have lost the war."

"Yes, I know. It's been on the news. Of the group, all did not get out clean. Apparently, four of them are being interrogated by the police right now. I'm not sure where this will all lead, but I suspect it will not turn out as well as we would like."

"I have the articles, Mr. President. Shall we call our confidential group together to review what we have?"

"Yes, and let's do it as soon as possible, tonight even."

"Very well, Mr. President, it shall be done."

The president's group met as planned, and the first thing was to distribute a copy of the articles to each of the members present.

The president opened the meeting by saying, "Gentlemen, before we go into the problems of what ended up being an unfortunate end to today's special project, it's important that we go through the articles. It will add perspective to how we proceed from here forward. Please now read what's before you and contemplate the meaning and let us then express our feelings about what the articles mean."

Silence fell across the room as each member read the articles. There were some moans and some expressions of anger and disbelief. But in the end, they each had something to say.

"The obvious disregard for the nation and its people for the sake of power is contrary to all that we stand for as a nation," said one.

Another said, "This is a conspiracy to change the order of governance in this country. How can we stand still and not act against such a ruthless and calculated plan to socialize this country in all its forms?"

And the last said, "It is my belief that when a group or faction plans to move in a deliberate immoral way to achieve power at any cost, it is imperative that an opposing force take away any opportunity for that force to succeed in whatever way seems necessary."

The president then said, "I agree with all your comments. However, we cannot go public with this for now for one simple reason: Nobody will believe it's true, and C3P will merely shout 'McCarthyism!'"

"Okay, Mr. President, how do we proceed?"

"I am not totally sure. It will need to be a process of counterintelligence and an effective action to counter the C3P goals. It will neither be easy nor short term because they have already gained impetus in their goals, and sadly, they are being successful. Perhaps, our day will come. It's going to take more than our little group to figure it out."

At this, the president then got into the immediate problems. "It looks like we are going to see fallout on today's activity at the office building. The arrest of part of the group is going to lead somewhere, and we are not sure just what yet. I suggest you gentlemen keep your ears to the ground and report anything that concerns you as to the impact to us or this office."

At this, the meeting was adjourned, and all went their way, all wondering just what would happen next. The president, left alone, started to read the articles one by one.

"Article 1—The end will justify the means, whether or not traditionally amoral or immoral.

"Article 2—The growing civil rights movement will be exploited for the party's own sake and not necessarily for the best interest of minorities or underprivileged. As a fact of history, give them what they can get for little or nothing, and they will obligate themselves to you. The general population will then support the party because Americans love the underdog.

"Article 3—The growing feminist movement must be exploited. By supporting them, it will foster planned parenthood and abortion. By furthering a general acceptance among the population, it will diminish the need for family unity and further the goal of government involvement in child welfare and population control.

"Article 4—Exploit the—"

At this point, the president put his head in his hands.

CHAPTER 10

The Fallout

President Sullivan had chosen a new director of the FBI. He chose outside the bureau, and this had a very negative effect on management within the department. In particular, it was offensive to the assistant director, who believed he was the legitimate heir to the outgoing director. Incensed by the selection and with a growing bitterness toward the president at his selection, he became increasingly vengeful in his emotions. And then it occurred to him. The incident at the office building housing the C3P national headquarters, involving a supposed fire, and the arrest of several individuals must have been the president's plan to gain information on the C3P. What better way to get back at the president than to leak a story to selected newspaper journalists? This event could lead back to the White House. It would give the president fits, and who knows where it would go if the right journalists took the bit and ran with it? Besides, if the president did initiate this break-in, isn't that an illegal act?

So, leaving his office, he went to a remote location where he could find a public phone. Calling the local newspaper, he asked for a journalist who was covering the office building fire where the C3P had their national headquarters.

"Who's calling?" said the party on the other end of the line.

"Never mind! Just put me through and I will give him or her some information that will be of benefit to whoever is pursuing a story on this case."

At that, a journalist was put on the line, "What have you got?"

The AD was adamant. "I will not discuss it on the phone, but give me a secure address, where I can send you this lead information, and then you can pursue it to its end."

The journalist gave him an address, and the phone conversation ended.

The assistant director, upon arriving at his FBI office, wrote a memorandum-style letter, indicating that "If the journalists plied their talents to investigating further, they might find that the break-in leads to the White House and the president. If they publicize their suspicions as a confidential leak from inside the government, they might get Congress to authorize a special investigation, and the C3P is sure to look at this as a strategic political advantage in once more putting it to their opposition. They will drive the call for the special investigation. In the name of responsible reporting, it is the duty of your paper to find out the truth. This comes from inside the government, so use this information accordingly."

When the letter arrived at the newspaper's confidential address, it was quickly taken to the editor who immediately assigned the receiving journalist the responsibility of pursuing the story to its end.

"Play it for all it's worth. You have the paper to protect your source, so find out what it's all about, look under every rock and if you can, find out who is the informant of this bit of news."

By now, The Committee, knowing they had the ATP by the "short hairs," began to play the media through their operatives like puppets on a string. The wheels of journalistic reporting began to turn and churn. First was the news item that says, "An unconfirmed and undisclosed leak from inside the government suggests that the break-in at the C3P national headquarters was instigated by the White House."

The White House responded by saying, "The article was irresponsible reporting, and there is nothing to support the allegations."

Then it was learned that one of the four break-in participants captured in the act was talking. It seemed he was an active member in the ATP at one time, with close ties to individuals in the CIA. It wasn't clear as to why he was talking, except he was apparently offered a plea bargain of some kind. In any case, this new information was enough for the C3P to call for a special investigation to get to the bottom of it all. It began to set the stage for a perfect opportunity to allow the C3P to go on the offensive against the present administration. The C3P quickly put their team of character assassins and propaganda forces to work, to get Congress to investigate the break-in.

For President Sullivan, the break-in news was taking a life of its own, and he was going to be swept into it one way or another. The distraction was going to take its toll. All he could do would be to deny his involvement and delay the process as long as possible. But, if he did deny it and evidence came forward to implicate him, he would be in an untenable situation.

The newspaper investigative reporters exhaustively worked the break-in story. Through follow-up on snippets of information from the secret source, the CIA director was drawn into the controversy. Finally, with so much attention drawn to the incident, it seemed there was enough smoke to make a fire, and an investigating committee was finally formed. Documents were subpoenaed including White House visitation records, which pinpointed several meetings with the president prior to the evening of and after the break-in. The president made a public announcement that he was not involved in the break-in, but enough information was being made available to cast doubt on his credibility. In the end, it looked like a solid case for impeachment, and the president was forced to make a decision.

So, with deep regret, the president announced to the world that he would resign, and the vice president would inherit his office. In utter disgrace, President Sullivan resigned from the presidency, carrying with him the secret of why the break-in occurred.

President Sullivan's VP finished out his term. The country, disenchanted with the ATP and its leader, responded to another "change" slogan, and CPPP successfully won the next presidential election. Once more, The Committee was able to enhance its opportunities through the C3P, and the new president made good on getting Congress to push through more programs designed to enhance the progress of socialism.

Under the new administration, one of the most far-reaching programs to affect the future of American economics was created. An additional government mortgage entity was enacted. This, along with an earlier agency, would serve to suck up a massive share of all mortgages in the country, forcing private sector equivalents to fight for their share by subverting their principles of common sense and financial discipline.

The new president of the C3P was well into his term of office. Despite winning his office as a backlash by the public, owing to the apparent lack of credibility of the outgoing president, the new president had little to offer. His administration saw the economy reach the highest level of inflation in recent memory, and interest rates went through the roof. Entitlement programs were in full force and making great demands on the Treasury. On top of that, the US witnessed the biggest hostage taking by a foreign nation when the US embassy in a Middle East country was raided by a segment of that nation's radical religious movement. The American attaches and embassy staff were held without legitimate cause. It was a culmination of inadequacy, failure to lead, and misguided micromanagement by the president and his staff. This failure in leadership and micromanagement came to its manifestation when a plan to rescue the hostages met with disastrous results.

The military concluded it had the ability to rescue the hostages by executing a plan to operate out of the desert. It meant flying in unnoticed, coordinating the rescue, and bringing the hostages back to the desert assembly area for flight out of the country. Instead of letting the military carry out the mission with experienced leadership and military expertise, the administration wanted the decision, as to when to deploy for rescue, to come from them and/or the president. This meant that decisions in Washington had to be made first for any departure of rescue helicopters and special force teams. With troops or personnel, C130 aircraft and helicopters massed in the middle of a desert thousands of miles away at night, waiting for decisions to come from Washington, was a disaster in the making.

At the supposed time for departure, the helicopters were started up according to plan for liftoff, but delays in the go-ahead from Washington caused the area to become a whirlwind of sand, dust, and disarray. When the first elements were about to take off, disorientation caused a helicopter to ram another, which then clipped a C130 on the ground. The helicopters crashed to the ground and immediately caught fire, and the C130 became involved as a crashing helicopter broke off the wing of the C130 spewing aviation fuel, which ignited into a mighty inferno.

Death and destruction were horrific, and the whole operation had to be aborted.

*****

Of all the candidates for office of president, the C3P's pick this time was all but acceptable to the general public. As his term of office ran out, it was obvious the C3P was going to have a hard time winning the next election, especially if the ATP had a candidate who exceeded previous candidates in personal charisma, charm, and the ability to communicate clearly with the people.

In the meantime, however, The Committee decided to review their present situation and analyze what their coming agenda needed to be. So, in the last year of their president's four-year term, they got together to review and solidify how to implement more articles. Also, a couple members of The Committee were getting on in years, and Ivan thought replacements had to be found. Twenty years had now slipped by since The Committee initiated their "Magna Carta," and this goal must be carried out to total fruition. So Ivan decided that decisions had to be made as to who would be the likely replacements or, rather, heirs apparent? The Committee met in their mountain compound, which, by now, they expanded to a wooded reserve of several thousand acres. With their lodge set in the middle, they maintained a secure setting with gated entry at only one strategic location. The perimeter was still patrolled by a security force twenty-four hours a day.

Meeting on this brisk, late winter evening, Ivan sat before this assemblage of aging zealots. He was always a large imposing figure, but after all these years, his features were exaggerated by his obesity. Now well over 350 pounds, he filled his chair and then some. His head showed no neck, and it set upon his massive hulk of a body without a hint of connection. He would clasp his hands over his huge stomach and, with a glaring look, view whoever was in front of him. His fat cheeks had drooped with age into jowls that looked more like dewlaps on an English bulldog. His lower lip would protrude outward, and his upper lip was imperceptible. With so much weight, he was always sweating. This caused him to give off an odor of perspiration mixed with lotion or deodorant. His large clear-rimmed glasses had slid down his smallish nose. Sitting there, he looked like a large, overstuffed owl. His scant salt-and-pepper hair, always damp with sweat, lay in stringy disarray. Even his peers, now present, had grown to avoid close encounters with him, not only because of his imposing personality but by his definite bodily exudation.

So, in a low, gravelly voice and a handkerchief clutched permanently in his hand to remove sweat from his brow, Ivan spelled out the meeting agenda. The last item on the agenda was to consider possible successors to this ignominious group.

Upon seeing the agenda, Casper insisted, "I'm not ready to give up my position unless I am on death's door. I'm finally seeing the fruits of my labor, and we're talking resignation? Oh no, I'm *not* ready!"

Merlin, irritated by Casper's outburst (he never really did like the "little pip-squeak"), bellowed back, "Why don't you shut up and wait until the item comes up on the agenda before you open your mouth? We all know you love your position of cloak-and-dagger."

Juno murmured, "I can't step down now. I'm in the middle of affecting changes in the C3P plan to influence the economy. I can't turn this over to somebody new at this stage!"

Ivan hammered on the table and bellowed, "Desist! We are not here to argue over our personal interests. We are here to continue our goal of implementing the Articles of Acquisition. If anybody is going to retire, it will probably be me."

There was a hush.

Ivan then proceeded, exclaiming, "We will talk about succession *after* we've discussed the first items on the agenda."

He then went on, "It's time to turn up the heat in the implementation of Article 5. As it says, we must debase the religious right and particularly the Catholic Church. Socialism has no place for religion."

Casper interjected, "Yes, Marx wrote that religion is the opiate of the people."

Merlin followed. "Yes, he knew that religion is the safe haven that people have traditionally used to salvage hope. They use God as their hope, and as long as they do that, they will not look to the state as their benefactor."

Ivan immediately responded, "Right! And, until the people begin to believe that the government is their savior in all things, they will be skeptical about a socialist system. Therefore, we must attack religion on all fronts. We must take it out of the public classrooms and workplaces. We must take it out of public buildings, parks, and any public subsidized environment. We must take God of our money. By removing religion, we dilute the existence of God. Once we do that, the people will come to realize that their real hope is in their government, who will look after them."

Standing up, Merlin said, "All the faiths are standing in our way, but our greatest antagonist in this regard is the Catholic Church."

"Why the Catholic Church?"

"There are sixty-seven million Catholics in the US. Their influence through the Pope, the church's position on contraceptives, fetal stem cell research, and abortion are examples of major factors that go against our philosophy. Our goal of calls for less God and more government control of lives is being thwarted as their bishops and priest direct a campaign to reject our goals."

Casper could hardly contain himself. He had a plan to weaken the Catholic Church in America. He said, "As you already probably know, Stalin initiated a program that sent his operatives into the United States, as well as other countries, to recruit candidates to enter into the Catholic seminaries and convents. This incorporated ordained clergy, committed to communism, into the church hierarchy. These priests and nuns would then work to subvert the church any way they could without being found out. Occupying visible positions within the church, they would assist in the hoped for destruction or diminution of the

Catholic faith by weakening its overall structure. We know that certain bishops, who are pseudoclergy operatives, are deliberately harboring priests who have abused young people or individuals by their predatory acts of sex. Their intent is to expose them at an opportune time. That opportune time is now!

"Additionally, we can do a great deal to influence a negative opinion of the Catholic Church in the eyes of the general population. We can use the Catholic fringe groups who are at odds with the church on several matters. These groups, which include some nuns and priests in defiance of their church's authority, must be infiltrated, encouraged, and supported. This will help create an atmosphere of doubt among the faithful. By using the media, especially the liberal media, and legal groups to identify and prosecute sex offenders, we do a public service and, at the same time, exploit the opportunity. By emphasizing degradation within the priesthood, we create more doubt in the minds of church members. By weakening the faith in their clergy, this insidiously weakens their faith in God. Additionally, it dilutes their trust in the precepts expounded by Rome when it comes to birth control, abortion, and the teachings of the church. The way the media eats up scandals, we should have no trouble propagandizing the whole matter."

Someone responded, "Yes, but all the faiths have had problems with clergy involved in sex crimes."

"That's true, but once we've made the Catholic Church and those damn Catholics irrelevant, then we go after the rest."

It was generally agreed that they would move forward to intensify the pressures on degrading reliance on God. Through the implementation of legal processes, all forms of reverence to God would be challenged. Casper was to implement plans, and Merlin would start the propagandizing process through The Committee's avenues of influence and media. Ivan then went on to the next article to increase an emphasis of action, namely, the unions.

"As article 7 describes, we must continue to encourage unionization of all facets of business, industry, and government. By supporting the unions, particularly the corrupt and mafia-influenced, they inevitably will be our enforcers in our new society. When all government agencies and all associated government departments are unionized, they become the shakers and movers to bend the general population to the government will. Furthermore, as the unions make bigger demands financially from management in the businesses they dominate, they weaken that business's ability to exist. They will require government bailout for industries with large employee forces and large financial obligations. They will become ripe for nationalization."

Merlin interjected, "Aside from the auto and steel industry, many businesses across the country either reject or there is a weak acceptance of unions within their companies. As a result, there is a general waning in unionization. However, in government, we are having more success in increasing unionization, and this should give us an edge in directing efforts toward a socialist system. We will continue to work with the unions through the C3P to protect them. With our political power in place, we will influence further support for union shops in businesses and union membership in government bureaucracies. As a source of revenue for us and with control over their members, they will see to promoting our candidates for office. They are an important ingredient to our success. Unionization of our educators will also go far in promoting our tactics through the educational process. For one, it will contribute to the diminution of religion through control of the classroom curriculum."

At this point, Casper chimed in by saying, "Article 9 says it best. 'Education is to be dominated by liberal educators so as to allow indoctrination of the tenets of a socialist system into the minds of our young people. It must start in government-controlled preschools and advance through the high schools."

Casper laughed excitedly as he said, "Yes, Hitler was extremely successful in fomenting an excitement and vigor into his Hitler youth to follow their nationalist system. If it worked for Hitler, it will work for us!"

He continued. "Colleges and universities that support liberal thinking must continue to be encouraged so as to develop within the minds of their students socialist ideals. The liberal colleges, universities, and institutions should be the source of advisors, drawn from the academic staff, to mentor our bureaucratic and political planners. I think you will all agree we must be relentless in making this happen."

Ivan now rapped on the table and said, "It's time to talk about succession in The Committee. To start with, I'm announcing my resignation as the last day of this year."

There was a gasp and then the usual "Why? What for? What's wrong? You can't. Are you ill?"

"The only thing wrong with me is my age. I'm getting old to the point of knowing it is time for a younger and more vigorous person to replace me. You all will have to face the same decision when you think it's right. Of course, you know my resignation is only of my position as C1 and not as a dedicated loyalist to our cause. Of that, I am eternally committed. As you all know, over the years since we started this movement, I have used my wealth to acquire, contribute to, and to underwrite many organizations in the support of socialism. This I will continue to do. This is where I will spend my remaining years, allocating my time and my financial resources to the cause. It is time now to decide on my successor. You all must think of prospective candidates to be considered. When we come to an agreement as to who it shall be, we will take the necessary steps to incorporate him or her into our group."

Over time, The Committee selected a replacement for the C1 position. That person had vast wealth and an idealist's view of a socialist system. He fit the essentials that The Committee was looking for. His leadership capability was obvious in that he had the bearing and forthright exuberance of a zealot. He accepted the baton of leadership and immediately set about the orchestration of things to come. The rest of The Committee followed his lead and instituted actions and policies that stimulated the C3P to action.

CHAPTER 11

A Dark Age Looms

When the ATP saw that the C3P's president in office was losing favor with the American public, they knew they had to come up with a candidate who would need to make a strong connection with the general population. Knowing that past candidates were strong in skills but weak in certain traits necessary to win an election, the ATP national committee held a meeting to review possible candidates. Assembling in their Washington headquarters, this meeting took on a serious tone.

Mike Michaels, the ATP party chairman, addressed the group. "Ladies and gentlemen, our next candidate for president of the United States must be someone who has the charisma, the force of speech, the leadership skills, and the background to win over the electorate. It's not enough that this person has past political skills or experience. This person must be able to help drive our party to a position of strength to overcome the excesses of our opposition.

The C3P has taken our country toward a precipice of unimaginable consequences. We must prevent any further strengthening of their base and reverse the tide."

The group then began the plan to vet potential candidates for consideration. Finally, after weeks of deliberation and several meetings, candidates were presented. One candidate stood out among the rest, meeting and exceeding *all* the party's requirements. His name was Richard Alexander Dawson.

Richard Dawson came from an average family. He went to college even though he only had an average record in high school. It wasn't because he was not smart; it was more in that he had a casual outlook on academic achievement. He did, however, like the art of debate, which he had dabbled in in high school and seriously approached in college. This helped him get through law school. Here he excelled, and upon graduation, he took a position with a West Coast law firm.

He was an astute and gifted attorney. With a mastery of speech and the ability to sway a jury, Richard Dawson became a star in the legal field. It didn't take long for his preferred party to recognize him as an ATP candidate for political office.

After serving as a state senator, he ran for the office of governor. He won. The people of his state gave him one of the highest percentages of voter approval over any other governors before him.

Richard Dawson became the ATP choice to run against the C3P. For once, the American Traditional Party was successful in having a candidate for the office of president who brought not only leadership experience but also an ability to connect with the public in charm, charisma, and wit. This, along with the country's general disgust with the C3P's candidate, proved to be enough to win the election, and the ATP came back into power. Almost immediately, the world changed in its appreciation of the forthright intent that the new president exhibited in his first days of office.

Richard Dawson's first order of business when entering his new position as president of the US was to decide what to do with the hostage situation in the Middle East. Gathering his cabinet for a special and secure meeting, he told the group, "The hostage fiasco has *got* to come to an end! The last administration has danced around this matter too long. It's time to get something done. I'm not going to beat around the bush. I want you to help me put in place an action plan I'm going to outline for you right now!

"First, it's obvious we are going to have to proceed unilaterally. Trying to do this through diplomatic action will take too long and may even mean death to the hostages, if some are not already dead, should we wait any longer.

"On the premise that they plan to kill the hostages anyway, we are going to take bold action. If we initiate a quick strategy, other nations that normally put up a fuss will not be able to react fast enough to make a difference.

"Therefore, here's what we do: I want to give this hostile country only twenty-four hours to release the hostages. If they refuse, we will exert immediate action. Delays and negotiation are not an option. We will send in a plane accompanied by fighter escort as soon as they accede to our demand. The hostages are to be put aboard our plane for immediate flight out of the country.

"Prior to our demand, I want to put all military on alert. Parallel to our demand, we do the following:

1. Where we have control, we seize or freeze all assets of this radical Islamic nation.
2. We put two aircraft carriers on station close enough to send our planes, with the intent that any aircraft sent aloft by this radical nation will be considered hostile and shot down.
3. We put as many submarines as necessary, within missile range of the country, to show our definite intent. We will not use a nuclear option, but the subs should be missile subs to give an indication of that possibility.
4. We advise all countries that they fly over the country in question at their own risk.
5. We put into the air long-range bomber units with the mission of bombing all military or civilian airport runways, if and when given the order.
6. We direct the Navy to establish the naval requirements to blockade all ships entering or leaving that country's ports.

"If they fail to accede again on the presumption that the hostages are dead or going to be killed, we will take the aforementioned action.

"I don't believe it will go that far, but if it does, let me say this: The taking of the hostages was an unwarranted and illegal act by a foreign nation. It doesn't matter that perhaps the group that took the hostages are a radical group. After this period of time, the country has done nothing to attain release of the hostages. Therefore, we consider this an act of war, and we will consider ourselves in a state of war if the hostages are not released. It is said that a just war is a defensive war. In this case, the best defense is a good offense. This offensive action is to protect our sovereignty as a nation in protecting the rights and lives of our attaches and embassy staff in a foreign country and to defend our right as a nation against overt unwarranted acts by hostile nations.

"Upon our consideration, I propose that the Secretary of State relay our intent, in specific terms, to this belligerent country.

"Prior to the secretary's presentation, we will inform the house majority and minority leaders of what we are about to do.

"Okay, that's it. I'm ready for discussion."

The first to speak was Andrew Cushing, the administration's new CIA director. "I believe the opportunity to accomplish this is very positive. At this moment in time, Russia is so caught up with economic problems that they have no interest in coming to the aid of anybody, least of all this country. Besides, with their mind set of "mutual destruction," it would mean facing a monumental decision. To them, it would be too much of a risk to get involved over this comparably minor incident. They wouldn't have the stomach for such a scenario."

Carl Plant, the Secretary of State followed by saying, "The regime in this country of question is relatively new. The type of action you're suggesting would be very overwhelming to them. They haven't the resources or the command-and-control capability to counter any action you propose to take."

General Doug Forster of the Joint Chiefs was present. "We can make all these happen. What time frame did you have in mind?"

"Two weeks," the president responded. "But I want all movements to take place covertly and to be in place on a designated date. I want to have the secretary inform their government so that they have the twenty-four hours to release the hostages—after everything is in place."

Somebody asked, "How do we react to the other countries when they kick up their fuss?"

"Simple, just ask them, 'How would you have acted to release your people?' I'm sure that will give them pause. Then say, 'What have you done up to this time to help us get our people released?'"

After much discussion, knowing the president was adamant in his intent to get this done even though there were some elements of doubt, they all agreed it was time to get the hostages out.

The military situated all necessary elements by the designated time frame, and the house majority and minority leaders were informed of the plan. The C3P railed against the plan, citing any number of consequences to this action. After their initial bluster, they saw that nothing was going to stop the action. Things were moving that fast, so they decided to let everything play out, and if it went wrong, they'd get their digs in afterward.

With everything in readiness, the Secretary of State was instructed to deliver the ultimatum.

Requesting an audience with the prime minister of the hostage-taking country and receiving approval to meet, Secretary Plant delivered his message: "Mr. Prime Minister, as we speak, your country is about to come under a state of siege initiated by the United States of America. Since you have found no urgency in releasing our hostages, we consider this failure to act as tantamount to an act of war. Therefore, we are making the demand that you release the hostages within twenty-four hours or things will automatically happen."

The secretary then spelled out the specific action that would take place if they refused and what they must do to remove the impending state of siege.

The prime minister paled in appearance. Stunned by this pronouncement, he could hardly speak. Then his demeanor changed, and he became visibly angry.

"How dare you confront me with such a ridiculous demand? Are you expecting me to accept this without exception? You know I can't do anything without the approval of my administration."

"Mr. Prime Minister, your country has twenty-four hours! No more! The time for diplomacy or negotiation does not exist in this matter. Either release the hostages or expect the consequence!"

In twenty-three and a half hours, the hostages were in the air on the way to the USA.

Now that the hostages were freed, the new president set his sights elsewhere; he made no bones about the country's position against the communist world.

After his first one hundred days in office, Richard Alexander Dawson was firmly into the daunting job of president of the United States. But he now was also much concerned about what was presented to him as the C3P's Articles of Acquisition. Soon after being inaugurated, one of his closest advisors and an ATP major operative told him that the force behind the C3P, directing all C3P policy, was a secret code of conduct in the form of a set of articles. These were instituted by a powerful enclave of individuals, working behind the scenes called The Committee. He was told that the ATP had acquired a copy of these articles, and the ATP would be looking to the president on guidance as to how to proceed.

Once the president read the articles, he knew action must be taken to counter this threat. But like his predecessors, he too felt that it could not be taken to the public. It would not be believed.

Acting upon his desire to implement some kind of counteroffensive, he called together his confidants: Jim Sykes, his political advisor; John Carlisle, his national security advisor; Carl Plant, his Secretary of State; and Gene Bates, a private industry consultant. In the meeting, all were advised of the articles.

The president said, "I am reminded of what Winston Churchill said at the outset of what would become World War II. I am going to repeat it now, but I will change some words to fit the present dilemma.

"'Upon this battle depends the survival of Christian civilization…Socialism knows that it will have to break our free enterprise and constitutionally alter our set of values or lose what they no doubt view as a war against a free democracy. If we can stand up to this menace, we will remain a free nation and the life of the world may move forward into broad, sunlit uplands. But if we fail, then the whole world, including this United States, including all that we have known and cared for, will sink into the abyss of a new Dark Age.'"

There was a surreal quiet that came over the room like a dark veil. And then, with a look of determination, Jim Sykes stood up and said, "We must create a creed to counter item for item what the articles lay out. Then we take a course of action to dispute and debase every one of the articles until they can no longer achieve their goal. It's not going to be easy, and we cannot do it just during terms of political majority. It must be done as long as is necessary until socialism is dead in this country."

One of this group immediately responded, "But some people view socialism as a necessary part of our democracy. They look at socialism as being compassionate toward the needs of mankind."

"What you say is true. That's how many view it, but they are confusing social responsibility with socialism. They are either unaware or ignorant of the fact that socialism is a 'system' that negates man. Human dignity is not part of socialism's creed. Socialism looks to man as the means to perfect the needs of the state. And those who promote socialism look to it as their means of acquiring power over men for the sake of an elitist group of which they will be a part."

The president said, "I agree. The best way to counter this threat is to find the antithesis to each article. Let's take each of them one by one and develop a countermeasure to destroy each article objective."

And so began the process to negate each of the Articles of Acquisition. Through several sessions, the group developed counterstrategies. They set about implementing a methodology to encourage traditional principles of freedom to downplay the articles.

As President Dawson's term of office developed and the successes of his administration took hold, the popularity of the ATP grew. Organizers within the hierarchy of the ATP were able to put together means and methods of strengthening the principles of a free democratic country. They established slogans and chartered groups to popularize their efforts, and gains were made.

The Committee, frustrated over the ATP president's rising popularity across the country, was in a state of agitation. So, in the wake of the successful extraction of the hostages from the Middle East and the movement by the ATP that was threatening the C3P's implementation of the Articles of Acquisition, The Committee members assembled at their mountain retreat.

Ivan opened the meeting. "We have a crisis in the making. Unless we find a way to mute the current president's ability to woo the population and attack our party's goals, we are facing eight years of the degradation of our objectives. This means a struggle that we may not be able to turn around. We cannot let that happen. Therefore, I am open to suggestions on how to proceed."

Casper, visibly agitated at the outcome of the hostage return and the rising popularity of the ATP, proclaimed, "Well, we do what we did with Cecil Howard. Permanent elimination would cause the ATP to scramble for leadership through their VP, who isn't exactly a stellar candidate for follow-up to the current president. This would weaken or, at least, delay efforts made by their party to counter the progress we have made."

Juno was not happy with the idea. "I don't believe another assassination will accomplish what you think! The sympathy acquired by this act on the part of the populace will endear them to the ATP even more. I think it would be a big mistake."

Merlin only sat and pondered what was discussed.

Then Casper, in a bit of a rant, said, "You know, Ivan, had you taken a more active role in the hostage situation by influencing our 'panty waist' president in the last administration to be more aggressive, we wouldn't be sitting in this situation right now."

Merlin agreed. "Yes, we blew it, and, Ivan, you played a big part in not making things happen."

Ivan, visibly irritated, charged, "Who are you to decide what I should or should not do? I suppose either of you want to be chairman of this committee. If so, stand up and make your intentions known."

At that, Casper stuttered, "Well-ah-that's not what I want. I just feel that we could have handled the situation differently."

"Oh yes, and just how would you have done that?"

Casper was about to give an answer when Merlin jumped in. "You could have persuaded our president to do what the current president has done. It's obvious his intelligence information was the same as ours."

Ivan didn't get a chance to answer.

Juno broke in. "Stop this arguing. What's done is done. It's not going to help our present situation. My suggestion is we let things play out a little longer before we take any specific action. Sometimes, things happen when you least expect. Who knows? Events might work in our favor."

Yes, events did unfold that not even The Committee expected.

*****

Abdul-Khaliq was born to a Middle East Islamic family with radical leanings and was indoctrinated by his parents at an early age. Their hope was that the religious clergy would be returned to leadership in their country and that the king-like ruler now in power would be removed or executed. All it would take would be for one of their exiled and revered Imams to be allowed back in. In preparation for this coming and to expand the education of their son, the family of Abdul dedicated him to an underground extremist group. There, armed with ferocity of a subverted Islamic spirit, he committed himself to unquestioned obedience to the leaders of this radical sect. Abdul was told by his mentors that there was going to be a zealous rededication to Islam, and he must go to the US. He was needed inside America to establish cells of believers like himself to be prepared to carry out special activities. The US was looked upon as the great Satan, and Islam must be established to unite all mankind under the umbrella of the Koran.

The day did come when the king was forced into exile. In his place, a charismatic Muslim clergyman was hailed back into the country to establish strict Islamic law. An emboldened religious fervor established rule over the nation.

Abdul, now in the US on an education visa and with freedom to move about, sought out Islamic centers of activity. He found a mosque in Niagara Falls, New York, that showed an obvious bent toward a more aggressive approach to Islamic action. Also, being so close to the Canadian border, it had escape opportunities if needed. Abdul settled in.

Not long after the US hostage rescue, Abdul received a message from back home. The message stated: "You are, in the name of Allah, hereby issued a fatwa to see to the removal of the president of the United States as punishment for his action against our holy nation. As your name implies, you are the 'servant of the creator,' and it is your destiny to carry out this command."

Abdul was enthralled. It was as if the message came from Allah. He must carry it out.

The first thing that Abdul did was to move to the Washington DC area. Then he began reading the newspapers and watching the TV station news to gather any knowledge of the movements of the president. This took some time, but he did see a pattern whenever the president was working in the White House. President Dawson had a favorite hotel restaurant that he frequented at least once a week for lunch. So Abdul would get up in the morning, travel to the area by bus, and walk to the hotel. He made a point of walking past every fifteen minutes or so until the hour approached when the president's entourage arrived. He then noted when he came and when he left. There were several days when the president didn't come, so his day was in vain. However, once he pinpointed several days that the president did come, he noted that he usually arrived by eleven forty-five and left usually by one thirty. He also noted that when the president left the hotel, the Secret Service men preceded him. Walking hurriedly, the president followed, surrounded by other Secret Service men or police officers. Sometimes, the press was present, and onlookers would yell to the chief executive. He often waved as he hastened to the limousine. Abdul knew, when the day came, he might have to take out several people to assure hitting his target. As to his fate, he never gave it a thought. He was on a mission as servant to Allah.

Now that he had established the pattern, Abdul decided it was time to purchase a handgun. This was done without difficulty. Having been trained back in his home country, he was familiar with how to handle all manner of weapons. An automatic pistol was his choice for this project.

All Abdul had to do now was to watch for the days the president would be in town. When that happened, Abdul would use his practice of walking past the hotel until the president arrived.

Abdul's day of destiny arrived. Walking toward the hotel, he saw the president's limo pull up and watched as the group headed into the hotel. Knowing the time that they would leave, he moved on and arranged his time to be back at the appropriate hour. Right on schedule, Abdul walked up onto the hotel just as the entourage was coming out. Secret Service men came first, then the president. On this day, onlookers were sparse, but there were policemen following closely behind the Secret Service men. This meant that if he was to get a clean shot at the president, he would have to cut down one of the policemen first.

Standing by a wall at the front entrance of the hotel, Abdul avoided notice as the Secret Service men came out to open the door of the limo. Seizing the moment, Abdul shot repeatedly at the officer who immediately fell. The agents reacted by spinning around, and Abdul shot repeatedly, killing one instantly, and shot again, wounding the other. The president, walking rapidly in his approach to the limo before the shots were fired, came into the line of fire and was hit once in the upper groin once the shooting began. By this time, police and the follow-up security men returned fire toward Abdul who was hit at least three times. He fell to the ground where he laid in a pool of blood. A police officer ran up to the downed assailant to see if he was still alive. Another officer following asked, "Is he still alive?"

"Nope! He's deader than a can of corned beef."

The president was literally thrown into the limo by the Secret Service agents. Speeding away from the hotel, the agents asked the president if he was okay. Stunned and not realizing he was shot, he said, "I don't know, but my stomach hurts." Looking at his face, they knew that he must have been hit, and they headed for the hospital. President Dawson was admitted in critical condition, and emergency surgery was performed.

The news flashed around the world: "The United States was shocked again as an unknown assailant attempted the assassination of President Dawson. Recovering at a Washington hospital, the chief executive is expected to have full recovery. Federal investigators are searching for answers."

It was some time before the president was off the critical list. In fact, if the truth were known, there was serious doubt as to whether he would make it. But to avoid panic and uncertainty in the nation and the world, this fact was never revealed.

The Committee, hearing that the nation's leader was shot, could hardly believe their supposed good fortune. Not having a thing to do with this deliberate action, it obviously took them by complete surprise. Somebody did their job for them. But though this act caused a slight pause in political events, nothing detracted from the president's popularity. Once recovered, President Dawson continued an agenda of positive accomplishments.

At the end of President Dawson's second term, the ATP politicians began to feel heady over the success of President

Dawson's two terms in office. The new president-elect had been an ATP candidate, and the ATP would continue in power, mainly as a result of President Dawson's successful administration.

Unfortunately, behind this facade of strength, there was the fateful dilution of dedicated party leadership, and there was the waning of a steadfast adherence to the principles of the American Traditional Party. The general population was beginning to feel that they were being taken for granted. The ATP leadership began to lose its way. Certain party leaders became enchanted by their newfound ability to become wealthy through positions of power. Ethics in the ATP began to lose importance, so by the end of what was a successful campaign and win by the ATP after President Dawson, the end of an ATP era was now in sight, and the C3P was about to regain power.

In four years and after twelve years of being in a position to make a big difference, the ATP saw their impetus slip away. Through persistent force from behind the scenes by The Committee, the C3P proved relentless in their war to bring about their socialist ideals to the public. The threat of socialism would now get an even stronger foothold.

CHAPTER 12

A Moral Meltdown

The Committee was ecstatic, the C3P won the presidential election, and the new president slipped one over on the populace by portraying himself as a moderate. His projection of charm and an ability to speak with a sound of assurance and honesty won the day. Little did the population know that what they were getting was a liberal with a socialist and a roué mentality. He was intelligent and extremely cunning. The truth was not necessary for him to accomplish what he intended. Lying was merely an expedient exaggeration to accomplish an end, and he used it with alacrity. It made for a dizzying eight-year term.

During the C3P's orgy of power, they managed to exploit every one of the thirteen Articles of Acquisition. Their latest effort was to implement with force article 13.

The party's new president, Thomas Augustus Bilkerton, proclaimed, "The environmentalists must be exploited by encouraging them to exaggerate the effects of mankind on nature. We'll encourage the environmentalists to direct their financial resources toward typically liberal environmental establishments, which can then be persuaded to direct these resources to our cause. We must join the international community in fostering a fear factor among the populace as to mankind's influence on climate change. By this, vast sums of money will have to be spent by industry, which will weaken its financial ability to compete and therefore make it easier to pull it into a nationalized structure."

The biggest boon to the C3P was putting the country's financial system into jeopardy through the quasi-governmental mortgage agencies established during the C3P's last period of power in office. President Bilkerton quickly saw to more liberalization of controls that were originally intended to manage prudent loan qualification. The idea now was to allow lower-income groups the opportunity of getting home loans easier, bring about the installation of political cronies into these mortgage agencies, have C3P representatives and senators influence political control over these cronies, and have this semipublic agency legally direct funds to lobbying groups who would support C3P efforts. Corruption crept into the whole system.

Corporate mortgage banking companies now found they were in competition with the quasi-governmental mortgage agencies. To prevent loss of position in the marketplace, they began to lower their standards. This led to corruption on the corporate level as fraud seeped into the whole process. Corporate executives, given to liberal ethics, soon found they would reap huge bonuses through massive increases in lending, packaging mortgages and selling them, thus raising profit, and then justifying bonus distributions to themselves. All because they loosened the standards and then exploited the process for all it was worth. Greed took hold as never before.

This era of power transformed the political landscape in a big way. With a liberal president now in power, with by all standards, a following of liberal attitudes, and a bent to increase the power of government, the traditional notion of "by the people and for the people" started to unravel.

Jim Cooper was still working at the White House, clearing candidates for positions in the administration. He was ever closer to retirement and planned this to be his last stint in federal service. He had seen several administrations come and go over the years, but this administration would make it easier for him to leave his profession and enter retirement.

On this particular day, he decided he would see his old friend and colleague Jack Watkins at the FBI office. Jack was also considering retirement. He never did get beyond his role of department supervisor probably because of his early contentious relationship with a certain assistant director of the FBI. Now he and Jim would commiserate over their years in the bureau and what they hoped the future would bring.

"Hi, Jack, what you up to?" Jim Cooper asked as he walked into Jack's office.

"Oh, not much, same old thing. How about you?"

"Same old routine. The outcomes are not really the same as they used to be. I do the background checks and offer my recommendations, and this new administration has the habit of taking candidates I would reject. They're taking people who have bad or questionable backgrounds and passing up those that have good, clean records."

Jack, still drawing on a pipe that had become a symbol of his persona, responded, "Yes, I wanted to talk to you about that. I'm getting a lot of reports from people wondering what kind of culture is developing over there. Things are sounding weird."

"Weird? It's getting downright eerie! The idea of a loose, freestyle atmosphere is being promoted, and it's downright debased. Professional courtesy is being abandoned. And as for dress and appearance, they are making a mockery of what has always been a level of high respect in dress and demeanor in positions of importance at the White House. The First Lady has little or no regard for military officers or staff members and makes it well-known. Administrative staff members known to be gay blatantly solicit for attention to willing others and similarly dress the part. There is no sense of organization or discipline, and there's no telling what's going on behind closed doors. It's scandalous to the extreme."

A spiral of blue pipe smoke wafted over Jack Watkin's head. With a transfixed look on his face, he stared out of the window.

"Well, Jim, I think you are going to see that this administration is going to be a lot different than the last in very dramatic ways. I happen to know that the president and the vice president are going to create a great challenge for us in toleration. They first showed their colors when they won the election. They were coming back from Miami and made a stop in Daytona Beach. I was informed that the Secret Service had to carry the vice president off the plane, and the president made it down the steps only with the help of two Secret Service agents. They were so drunk they had to make their arrival secret. You will note that the press corps did not report this incident because they were too inebriated and could hardly report on something they were a part of. The only people who witnessed all these were baggage handlers at the terminal and, of course, our people."

"Well, Jack, I can only say that I will be very glad when I can retire. With The Committee implementing its fullest intent and the opposition seemingly unable to convince the general population that socialism is threatening to dominate this country, I shudder to think where it's all going to end."

"Yes, Jim, you and me both."

The C3P did their best to debase all the notions of traditional government. The Constitution was under attack (e.g., freedom of speech, freedom to bear arms, freedom of religion, and anywhere that Constitutional rights could be challenged). With all operatives armed with the Articles of Acquisition, the C3P attacked everything and everyone to achieve their socialist ends.

However, the weakest link in their control of power was their president. His demented involvement with women was not only his but also the C3P's undoing. Into the second term of the presidency, his sexual activity in the White

House proved too much. The House of Representatives recommended impeachment.

During the impeachment process, President Bilkerton's counsel, White House advisors, C3P members of the House, and Senate rattled on about how the president was being treated unfairly. Finally, out of disgust, a distinguished ATP senator managed to get before his colleagues in the Senate to vent his frustrations over the subject of "fairness."

"My distinguished colleagues, the findings by the special prosecutors as relates to President Bilkerton are being labeled as unfair. Presentations by the house managers on the impeachment trial are being called unfair. This is about not what pertains to the office of president but of Thomas Augustus Bilkerton, one person elected by the people of the United States of America to be leader for this country and who is a symbol of leadership in the world. It has also been put before the people of this country that the charges to convict the president of perjury and obstruction of justice on actions that seemingly do not rise to the level of *high* crimes and misdemeanors according to the Constitution offer no basis for conviction. But I say here that if the office of president of the United States is the *highest* office in the land, how can it follow that if the person occupying this *high* office commits perjury or the obstruction of justice, for whatever reason, that it is *not* a *high* crime or misdemeanor? *High* office such as that of the presidency, by its very name, means a position of influence over all the elements of our government and society as a whole. Nothing is diminished in the exercise of that office in its power and precedence before the nation and the world. Abuse within that office should not be tolerated whatever the form.

"So I beseech you ask yourself these questions:

1. When Thomas Augustus Bilkerton had an 'improper relationship' while occupying a public office with a public employee in a public building during and after working hours, was this fair to office of the president of the United States and the American people?

2. When Thomas Augustus Bilkerton had his 'improper relationship' in a public environment and members of his staff, counsel, and political associates led you to believe that this was a personal and private affair, was this fair to that office and the American people?

3. When Thomas Augustus Bilkerton went before his cabinet and staff members and denied having a relationship with a White House staff member, was this fair to that office and the American people?

4. When Thomas Augustus Bilkerton had an 'improper relationship' while occupying his high office and brought discredit to that office and aid and comfort to those nations who threaten

great harm in the world, was this fair to
that office and the American people?

"I ask you! What is fair? The health and welfare of
Thomas Augustus Bilkerton? Or the present and future
health and welfare of our country and the American people? Where is the greater good served? The individual who
has abused his office of responsibility or preserving the
sanctity and credibility of the office of president? There is
only one answer, and in this case, it means the removal of
Thomas Augustus Bilkerton! This office is not expendable.
The person occupying that office is! This nation has endur-
ing strength through adversity but will crumble under the
weight of internal corruption and abuse of office. The brick
and mortar of this nation are the moral and legal codes of
righteous men and women who uphold the intent that all
laws apply equally to all, regardless of office, so help us
God!"

Despite all the rhetoric to oust the president, there was
enough support to defeat impeachment.

But the country and its citizens had enough. The C3P
lost the next presidential election.

The Committee immediately consolidated their efforts
to continue their attack on the American democratic system. Having made great strides during the past eight years,
they had established a huge network of organizations to
support their cause. Using every scurrilous means available
to them, they managed to develop a socialist movement
that just needed another opportunity to acquire political
power.

Due to the disappointments of the last election, The Committee decided they needed to "beef up" their ability to control the elections. So they set up another meeting to contemplate the subject of generating more cash for the C3P for distribution to neighborhood enclaves to get out the vote and for special political ploys. Not particular as to how or where it came from, everybody was queried as to ideas on how to come up with more cash.

Ivan prodded. "Certainly, with all our contacts, we can find a means to shake loose capital from somebody? Is there anyone we could squeeze?"

Juno was listening, and it was obvious her mind was working. Then, with a smile, she said, "When I was working in the financial field, I was struck by the fact that there was a certain investment company returning high yields to its investors. These yields were out of pattern to typical returns in the marketplace, and it occurred to me that this consistency of return was too high to be legitimate. I didn't dwell on it at the time, but this company has since grown to a multibillion-dollar operation, including all its affiliations. For some reason, they have stayed under the radar of scrutiny by the SEC, but I'm sure there's something funny going on."

Eyes wide, Ivan charged C2 with getting the backup. "Casper, get your moles to look into this and report back to us. Once you get the goods on this company, have Juno review the detail, and then we get Merlin involved to put on the 'touch' and Juno to work on the movement of cash."

Ivan liked the sound of this. But he wanted more possibilities.

Merlin suggested, "There are certain other megamillionaires or billionaires who are now out of the country due to legal issues facing them in the US. I'm sure we could shake them down in return for clemency by any president we have in office. You saw how well it worked with our last president, why shouldn't it work again?"

"I like that. Let's put it together and see where it goes."

Casper found that the company Juno had suspected of funny dealings was still involved in what appeared to be questionable activity. Bringing the data they had gathered from internal company sources to Juno for scrutiny, she wasted no time in identifying the fact that this company was nothing more than a giant Ponzi scheme. The "top dog" in the company was living "high on the hog" with expensive cars, homes in two foreign countries, and a $10,000,000 yacht. He had a multimillion-dollar penthouse in New York and was funneling money to all his immediate family. He looked like a perfect "patsy" for extracting funds. It was now the time to weave the web and pull the victim in.

CHAPTER 13

The Spider's Web

Landon Albemarle built his financial empire on the concept of a Ponzi scheme right from the beginning. He knew he had to go for fast growth at the outset to keep enough money in front of him to continue to entice his investor clients. Having worked the financial market for many years, he knew how things worked and how to evade detection by the regulatory agencies. In a matter of ten years, he was amassing millions of dollars and attracting some of the wealthiest individuals and public and private retirement funds. The flow of cash was so great that he had no trouble finding the ways and means to skim what he wanted for his own personal needs and wants. Particularly his wants.

Moving around the country and the world with his massive financial arsenal, he stayed within the realm of the rich and famous. This included summering in the Hamptons, attending lavish cocktail parties and various gala functions. It was at one of these parties that he met a very interesting and mysterious gentleman. Unbeknownst to him, this gentleman was not a gentleman but a clever member of The Committee. Merlin, through his old contacts, managed to make his way back into the mix of the Hampton aristocracy. Finding Landon was easy, as he was well-known for his supposed philanthropic activities, and he too put on lavish parties.

It was at a beachfront estate afternoon cocktail party that Merlin sidled up to Landon. "Mr. Landon, my name is Jacob Brockmorton. I am the fund manager for a large state pension fund. I am looking for a place to put our investment resources. It constitutes hundreds of millions of dollars, and we need a better rate of return. I understand your company provides attractive returns, and I need to discuss the possibilities. I am only interested in talking with *you* on this matter. I will feel better if we do this one on one."

Although Landon was not always involved in the day-to-day acquisition of new clients, this big source of revenue intrigued him, so he had no trouble in responding. "Of course, Mr. Brockmorton."

Merlin, under the guise of Jacob Brockmorton, said, "Call me Jake. No need for formality. From what I'm told, your expertise and style makes you the kind of person I like to work with. Therefore, you and I should get along very well."

Landon, now having taken the bait, said, "Of course, Jake. Can I get you something to drink?"

"No, thanks, I've got a drink here somewhere. I would, however, like to get someplace where we can talk with less activity going on."

"Certainly. Let's go by the window. There's less going on over there, and there's even a table for our drinks."

As they both sat down, Merlin suggested that Landon consider coming to his hotel room later.

"I've brought with me all the investment data you will need to put a package together for us. It's pretty comprehensive, so, obviously, you will need to look at it. You can take it along with you after we meet. I want you to know that it is a very substantial amount of money, and we must assure ourselves that your returns are as lucrative as we've been led to believe."

Landon's curiosity was high, and he needed to see this package. *Were there millions or closer to a billion?* he mused. He was going to have to find out. So he said, "I'll be glad to come to your room. We can go now, if you like?"

Merlin said, "No. Why don't you come around nine o'clock tonight? I'll have refreshments, and we'll be able to go over the details then." Merlin gave Landon the name of a plush hotel he was staying at, excused himself, and left.

That evening, Landon knocked on Merlin's hotel room suite precisely at nine o'clock. Surprisingly, it was not Merlin who came to open the door. It was a professional-looking woman dressed in business attire. Also, there were two big men, similarly dressed. They looked more like bodyguards than businessmen.

"Please sit down, Mr. Albemarle. Thank you for coming. We have a lot to talk about."

Landon became nervous. Something was not right about this meeting, and he wondered, *Why all the people?*

"I thought I was meeting Jake at this meeting. Why the extra people?"

At that point, Merlin entered the room. "Relax, Landon. We are here to make it clear as to what is all involved in your relationship with us. After all, you wouldn't want us to become associated with each other if there wasn't something to gain for all parties in this relationship. You get to continue your financial empire, and we get to use you as an important means to acquire funds."

Landon could see that he was facing something entirely different than he had imagined.

"What are you talking about?"

Merlin, with a wry smile on his face, said, "I'm talking about the fact that you get to keep running your giant Ponzi scheme, you pay us a stipend at our discretion, and we'll see to it that you are protected from scrutiny by regulatory agencies. We are a big organization, Landon. We are not to be messed with."

"Ponzi scheme! What Ponzi scheme?"

"Oh, come on, Landon. We know all about it. We have internal documents and data from your business that verifies what kind of business you are running. In the wrong hands, this information would collapse your entire organization."

Landon went into a cold sweat. "What do you want from me?"

"We want money, Landon. Lots of it!"

"How much?"

"Well, let's see now. How much did you pay for your yacht? Ten million dollars?"

"What's that got to do with it?"

Merlin, now seeing he'd gained the desired attention, replied, "That is exactly the sum you are going to give us each year of a major election. You will have the privilege of knowing that you are contributing to a worthy cause."

"Ten million dollars? Are you crazy? How do I get that much out of the company?"

"How did you get that much out of the company for your yacht? Or for that matter, how do you subsidize all your family members, the homes, and the cars you've bought? No, Landon, if you figured how to do that, you'll also figure out how to hide another ten million dollars. After all, you have no choice. Accept this arrangement or your business empire dies. And if it dies, you will die with it. In jail!"

After all the years of arrogantly sitting on top of one of the biggest financial businesses in America, Landon was now facing blackmail and ruin. His choice, reluctantly arrived at, was no surprise.

"As you say, I have no choice. But first, I want to see proof that you really do know what's going on in my business. I am not stupid enough to just take your word."

The woman sat down next to Landon with a thick file. As she pulled page after page of obviously incriminating information, Landon got angrier and angrier, but he managed to maintain his composure and resigned himself to the fact that he was completely trapped. Knowing his goose was cooked, he said, "What and when do you want it?"

At this point, the woman relayed her instructions. She began. "You will transfer monthly sums to a bank we have selected in the Bahamas. We will tell you the date to do it, and you will do it every month for a year. If we elect to change the receiving bank, we will let you know. The sum will be one twelfth of the ten million dollars each month. This you can expect to do every two years, once for off-year elections and once for presidential elections."

Curious at the interval, Landon questioned, "Why the monthly amounts?"

She responded, "We have our reasons. Besides, smaller amounts are less visible in your organization. I would think you, of all people, should know that."

"Yes, yes, you're right," he said resignedly.

Landon's frustration with the matter was getting to him, but there was no way out of this disaster. He was caught in the web.

"For now, this meeting is over. Don't expect to see any of us again. You will be contacted by courier with instructions on when and where to transfer funds. Treat these instructions with absolute immediacy. Any delay on your part will bear consequences you can only imagine."

Landon left the hotel psychologically exhausted; he was finally caught. He never thought he would be caught by unknowns; he always thought that if it did happen, it would be the feds. Were these people mafia? He could only guess. In any case, they had him, and he intended to follow through on their demands.

And so it was. When the year came for elections, money was wire-transferred to a Bahamas bank. An agent of The Committee would withdraw the money in cash. This agent would arrive in the Bahamas by a recreational fishing boat. Once the money was brought aboard, the fishing boat would head for any of a number of Florida coast cities. Here the funds would be divided for transfer by courier to Chicago, Detroit, New York, and anywhere cash could be utilized to pay for a turnout of the vote for the C3P. Whether it was paying for motivating registration, busing voters to voting stations, or hiring demonstrators for political purposes, cash was used to eliminate traceability. And, whenever cash was withdrawn from the Bahamas bank, the account was closed, and a new offshore account was set up elsewhere. Money laundering was an important consideration in avoiding any linkage to the instigators of this scheme.

Poor Landon, he didn't know it then, but he would be subsidizing the end to his entire financial fantasyland.

CHAPTER 14

Squandered Chances

Albert Bunson of the American Traditional Party won the next presidential election. It wasn't long, though, before a crisis that was in the making during the previous administration manifested itself. It was no coincidence that an attack on a financial center was carried out by the group of terrorists who had been training in the Middle East. This dastardly execution of thousands of innocent Americans was possibly the result of failure to act at a crucial time by the former president. There was no proof to indicate that fact because insufficient investigative data never brought out the probability. Curiously, many records of the previous administration had mysteriously disappeared during the transition of power. Therefore, the suspicion always existed that an event had occurred that lent credence to the possibility of dereliction of duty.

This assault by a Middle East terrorist organization involved the murder of thousands of innocent citizens in what was a carefully planned bombing attack. Immediately, the nation went into panic mode, as several incidents occurred at the same time elsewhere in the country. For the first time in a long time, the nation became united in its efforts to defend itself against such outside forces. The new administration was immediately consumed into establishing the mechanisms to protect its great nation.

President Albert Bunson was an inarticulate president who won his party's nomination because of his political background, his seemingly prudent past, and his generally likeable nature albeit the fact that his mastery of speech-making bordered on the equivalent of a freshman high school student trying out for the forensics team. The voting public elected him primarily because of the embarrassments of his predecessor in office. He also gave a general projection of credibility throughout his political career, having served as governor of a major state. His qualities were sufficient, especially his dedication to seeing to the safety and security of the country, and to that, he was a bulldog, often inviting severe criticism from the other side of the aisle and foreign nations. However, he had to deal with a country now being influenced by the C3P's constant move toward big government and its growing network of organizations willing to dedicate its resources to the establishment of a greater socialist movement. In this, President Bunson never seemed to be willing to acknowledge or project to the American public in a forthright way.

The nation was facing not only an outside threat but there was also a threat from within. This threat was challenging the constitution and the structure of the country.

He instead left it up to his party to carry the ball in challenging the opposition. He dealt with the day to day, often conscientiously trying to work with members of the opposing party, usually to no avail. Unfortunately, his party, drunk with the elation of being able to serve two terms, was too busy wallowing in its own power. Many of the ATP leaders were too busy lining their pockets with special interest gratuities. Even former political leaders, now having lost reelection or retiring from service, set their principles aside and were starting to buy-in to the idea of bigger government. They began to support causes through lobby positions, often supporting issues contrary to what were once their traditional convictions. This allowed the C3P to gain greater foothold, influence their cronies in office or in the bureaucracies, and implement policies that would lead to an inevitable economic crisis of huge proportions.

After eight years, a period of time when the ATP should have solidified their political and moral stance, the country instead entered into an era of domination by the C3P. The ATP was defeated by a socialist who amassed popularity through a carefully crafted campaign. He brought with him a Senate and House putting the C3P in control. The new president could now move the country toward overt socialist development. The whole nation was under attack by powers to reshape and reform the system and to negate the Constitution of the United States. The economic state of the country was so critical that the regime saw its opportunity to aggressively bring about the release of huge sums of money into a system with obfuscated means and methods of allocation. By this, they gained access to funds that could not be adequately tracked or reconciled, thereby directing it where they wanted to enrich some and empower others to the benefit of the C3P. They had a new financial means to implement a socialist agenda to fullest intent.

Truly, the Articles of Acquisition had instituted their movement, and they were about to bring it to fruition. The Committee's Magna Carta had laid the framework, and the C3P was carrying it out. Now it was just a matter of completing the task.

At a meeting of The Committee, Ivan expounded. "We have climbed the mountain of opportunity and have made it subject to our destiny. We must now begin the process of total transformation. It is time to fundamentally transform America into a nation of leaders and followers. Leaders who will make the rules, followers who will do our bidding. In this, we will preserve power for the elite and protect the followers from themselves by making them all equal. This will be our perception of justice carried out, one nation by the state, for the state, with liberty and justice according to an elite hierarchy, administered according to our will."

In the first year of the new administration, the C3P boldly entered into a process that was clearly socialist in nature. Incorporating individuals with known liberal/progressive, socialist, and communist convictions, these individuals became part of the administration. Catering to the establishments and wealthy individuals that embraced their philosophies, they proceeded to openly push for policy changes that would challenge democracy through an implementation of socialist principles. They moved to nationalize health care and the automotive industry and to bring the banks and the fed under the thumb of strict and absolute control of the government. Bureaucrats would now make decisions for these entities whether the general population liked it or not. The president, no longer acting as a servant of the people, spoke and postured like a dictator of a communist nation.

The ATP, now out of power, recognized the need to expose the C3P for what it was. It was just a matter of how and when.

For two years, the C3P managed to continue to pursue and implement in whatever way they could, socialist control. Not surprisingly, the general population was beginning to react against such blatant moves to institute an all-powerful central government. The C3P was beginning to lose public support to such an extent that candidates and office holders were weakened in their attempts to seek reelection or to carry out certain agenda. Perhaps, a new breeze was blowing over the country, and people were beginning to realize that their freedoms were threatened. The C3P, shaken by this sudden reverse in public opinion, needed something to happen. But what?

CHAPTER 15

A Diversion

The Committee called a special meeting. The nation was reacting negatively to the C3P, and it was showing in the polls and the voting booths. So a diversion of major impact was needed to regain the confidence of the masses.

Ivan began. "We need a diversion. Something big to rouse the population. Something that will further our cause, alert all to the dangers of capitalism, free enterprise, and man's impact on the environment."

Casper had an idea. "We all know that the oil industry is huge and powerful. We know that they are the epitome of capitalism, and I believe we all agree they need to be nationalized to further our intents. Therefore, we create a calamity of such massive proportions that a major oil company and the environment are put at risk. The end justifies the means, article 1. We put the hit on a drilling rig, and the environmental damage that results will force the company to its knees. We will have to seize its assets and run it.

"In 1979, the oil platform Ixtoc burst into flame and collapsed. Tens of millions of gallons of oil gushed into the Gulf of Mexico. It took ten months to stop the leak and spewed a record of 140 million gallons of oil into the sea. Shorelines in Mexico and Texas were affected.

"If we can hit a drilling platform in a way to create a spill that mirrors or exceeds Ixtoc, we will have our diversion."

Juno was particularly irritated by this suggestion. "Are you telling us that we should ruin the environment, kill several people, and possibly put our position at risk for the sake of creating a diversion? It seems to me if this went wrong, we wouldn't gain in our efforts. We would lose! Big!"

"You are missing the point! Because of the environmental implications, the people will see the government as the only one who can solve the problem. Secondly, there will be a call for the government to seize control of the company and its assets. It can be claimed that it's the only way to see to the proper distribution of funds for cleaning up the mess. If we respond to this call and perform in a timely manner, we can reverse the present negative sentiment toward the party. Further, we reinforce the necessity to nationalize our control of businesses."

"And if it goes wrong?" Ivan responded.

"It's a bet we have to make or we lose badly in the next election, which could reverse all our efforts so far." Casper was adamant.

"Have you an outline of a plan of execution that you can offer?"

"Yes, I do."

"Let's hear it."

"We find a person with scuba experience who has a grudge or radical desire to get back at the oil companies. We work out a sea drop to get him close enough to the rig to swim to it. Using a high-impact explosive device, he will set off the demolition under the rig on the well pipe at the water level. When it blows, it should immediately catch fire and envelope the whole platform."

Someone replied, "What happens to the scuba diver?"

"He will be incinerated. Actually, he will be vaporized. Of course, he will think it's a timed fuse with enough time for him to get away, that we will pick him up at a safe distance, and that he can take a long vacation with one million dollars. No witnesses."

Juno, wearing a look of foreboding, made her feelings heard. "You guys always think that the only way to eliminate a problem is to liquidate or exterminate. There is a time and a place for that sort of thing. I just don't think this is it. The risk is too great, and the collateral damage is huge."

Merlin, on the other hand, seemed to think it was worth the chance. "Look! When this thing happens, as the leak begins to threaten the shorelines, there is going to be a big to-do about getting the leak stopped and who's going to pay for the clean-up. The idea is for us to convince our cohorts in office to drag their feet on government assistance, point the finger instead at the oil company, who should be held responsible, and force them to pay the tab for clean-up and restoration. The public will cry for blood and actually encourage the government to take over the industry. As time goes on, the company will lose billions, and their stock will fall like a stone. The administration can then seize the company as a failed entity since it no longer has the viability to carry its responsibility. It will be another step closer in nationalizing business."

Juno was still doubtful. "Yes, if all goes according to your crazy plan. But what if doesn't? What if the nation turns against the administration for failure to act? That could be the nail in our coffin."

Merlin looked Juno in the face. "You just can't see where this will go if it succeeds. It will succeed if we want it to. My bet is we can make it work, and it's worth the shot."

Ivan took it all in as argument upon argument moved back and forth. In the end, Ivan made the decision. "We have to go for it! It's the only way that we have a chance of turning public opinion back in our favor. Yes, the risk is great, but I see it as there is no other choice. It's going to take a big event, short of an outbreak of war, to gather the nation's attention. If we can hold that attention through these elections, we will hold the majorities we need to get more time to solidify our political positions before the next election."

Casper was instructed to proceed, and he immediately went to work.

*****

Joe Fox was a rough and tumble kind of guy. He lived a worry little, carefree life. Built big and strong, he found himself working in the steel yards, welding on oil rigs for the big oil companies. The money was good and the work demanding. He spent the money as fast as he made it, drinking, womanizing, or exploiting his favorite pastime: scuba diving. Traveling around, he would go on spearfishing jaunts or search for underwater treasures. The latter was a passion. Unfortunately, he never succeeded in finding anything but a few trinkets and relics that were of little or no value. To find the real treasure would take a lot of money, and he didn't have it, so he confined his interest to fishing and dabbling for undersea paraphernalia.

Then an event occurred that would change his life. Joe worked for the same company for many years until one day, while working on a drill rig, Joe was required to assist, by hand signal, a crane operator in the lifting of heavy plate steel into an upright position for welding. His immediate supervisor, who normally did this, had directed Joe to help in this case even though Joe was not properly trained for that type of activity. With Joe using rudimentary signals, the crane operator misinterpreted the signals and let the steel plate come down suddenly, crushing Joe's working partner, killing him on the spot. It was a traumatic event that Joe had trouble getting over. But the big problem was that the supervisor blamed Joe and lied in denying he ever instructed Joe to assist the crane operator. The supervisor convinced the oil company that Joe was a "loose cannon," that he created ill will among the workers and frequently avoided safety procedures. Despite Joe's insistence that he was a victim of circumstances and after hiring an attorney to defend himself, the corporate attorneys were too big an obstacle to overcome. The company had to show negligence directed toward one individual to save face. Joe lost his case and was fired, and his reputation preceded him wherever he tried to find work. He became desperate and carried with him a big grudge against the oil company that wouldn't back him up.

Casper had put the word out to his operatives in the dock areas of the gulf coast that he was looking for someone who had talents in scuba diving activity. Finding the right person would be a long shot. So he used the union halls in the area to get feedback since this is where he had his closest association. Word eventually got back to him about this guy Joe Fox. He was known to sleep at a shelter and eat at the local handouts. Casper immediately jumped on the opportunity to get Joe for his project.

Joe Fox had just finished eating supper at the local food kitchen. It wasn't bad either: beef stew, potatoes, corn on the cob, and all the iced tea he could drink. It didn't cure the hate, however, that still swirled around in his head. If he had a way to get back at the oil company, he would do it. But how could he? He was nothing compared to them. It would have to be big. Even so, he just didn't know what he could do to make a difference.

It was then that a big black SUV pulled along the curb next to him. The power window went down, and the driver inside said, "Hi, Joe, how are you doing?"

Joe, startled, looked at the driver. "Who are you? What do you want?"

"Your buddies said you are having a rough time and need a job. I've got something you might be interested in."

Joe could hardly believe it and couldn't help but be a bit suspicious.

"Yeah, well if you know about me, you probably know I'm blackballed around here. Why would you want to use me?"

By now, the driver had opened the passenger door.

"Well, my job requires your special talents. It's not in steel. It's in scuba diving."

Joe's heart leapt. Could this be for real?

"Scuba diving! That's right up my alley. What have you got?"

"Get in and I'll take you to someone who will tell you all about it."

After driving and talking for a while, the driver stopped at a motel. "Here's a key. Go to room 107. It's up front on the first floor. Your visitor will drop in on you in about an hour. In the meantime, you might want to take a shower. There are clean clothes in the closet. They should fit. I left a bottle of good whiskey on the bathroom counter, and there are some beers and good mixes in the fridge. Help yourself to whatever you want."

"Wow! Never got to interview for a job like this before," Joe said to himself.

No sooner did Joe get out of the SUV, it was gone. So he walked to the room and let himself in. Everything was as the driver said. With an hour to spare, he cleaned up, poured himself a tall whiskey straight, and crawled onto the bed. Propping up a couple of pillows, he turned on the TV and took in the start of an old movie. With a long gulp of whiskey, his body shuddered as the potent elixir found its way to his stomach. "Whoa, but that hits the spot." He was starting to feel good about himself again.

After an hour exactly, there was a knock on Joe's motel room door. Joe approached the door, trying to imagine whom he would be facing. Upon opening the door, he was stunned. Standing before him was a very striking and healthy-looking woman. Almost six feet tall, she looked like a very athletic equivalent of a professional tennis player or bicyclist.

"Hello, Joe," she said in a firm but seductive manner.

"Uh, I mean, yah—hello!" He kind of faltered backward as she entered the room.

"Don't get any wrong ideas, Joe. I'm here strictly on business and not the business you might be thinking right now."

"You mean *you* are going to interview me for this job?"

"You got it. And I might tell you that if this works out, it's worth one million dollars to you in cash."

"One million dollars, you've got to be kidding me." He grabbed his whiskey glass and filled it. "Can I offer you a drink?"

"No, thanks," she responded.

One million dollars, oh, could I ever start my own treasure-hunting business with that? he opined to himself. But then his instincts kicked in. There must be a gimmick. No one offers that kind of money unless they want some dirty deed to be done. "All right, what's the gimmick? No one gives out that much dough without something big in return. What's the deal?"

Sprawling herself on the bed, she displayed lots of leg, and with a suggestive look, she replied, "How do you feel about your old employer?"

The whiskey now working on Joe's brain, combined with the thought of his old employer, triggered rage deep within him that spewed upward. His face contorted into a demonic expression of hate. Turning toward the woman, he raged, "If ever I get the chance to get back at them, I will do anything to get satisfaction."

"Anything?" she said.

"Yes! Anything!"

"Okay, I'm giving you that opportunity. But you should know that since you've come this far, there is no turning back. My people offer deals you can't refuse. Denying them is fatal. You will get your million dollars. I will bring you $250,000 in cash on the day of what we call the day of deliverance. This will prove to you we are serious. The balance will be in a locker at a specified railroad station. The key for the locker containing the balance will be with the quarter million. This downpayment will stay in your motel room, so when we have completed the job, we can return to the motel where you can collect your cash, and we will go our separate ways. After that, you can pick up the rest of your reward at your convenience."

Suddenly, Joe realized he was trapped. But, what the hell, where was he going anyway?

"Okay, so give me the lowdown. What am I doing? How does scuba diving come into all these?"

Sitting up on the bed, she laid out the plan. "We have acquired a fishing boat. You and I will take that boat out within proximity of what so happens to be an oil platform operated by your old employer. We are going to take that platform out. Why? Let's just say it fits into the plans of your new employer."

"Oh yeah, and just how do you expect we are going to take it out?"

"We do the job at night. You will snorkel and scuba to the platform, place a high-impact charge on the well pipe just above the waterline, and return to the fishing boat. With the ruckus created by the explosion, we will disappear into the night. The charge will have a timed circuit to go off thirty minutes after you flick the switch. That should give you plenty of time to get away from what should be a brilliant display."

Joe asked, "You know that platform is lit up like a polish church? With all those lights, they will undoubtedly see me."

"Yeah, that's possible, but doing it late means that whoever normally watches is probably not going to pay much attention. Besides, there are always a lot of fish swimming around under the platform in that light, and you might not be as obvious, especially if you come up from the depths alongside the well pipe. Worst case, if they spot you, you probably could evade them in the dark waters away from the platform because it will take some time to get down and into a boat to seek you out. Their only thought about you will be that you are a spear fisherman trying to do some night fishing around the platform."

"All right, but how do I get that much explosive to the platform?"

"We've taken care of that. Your scuba gear will have two tanks, one for your scuba and the other will be packed with explosive. The tank with the explosive will have the timer included. That's why you need your snorkel, and you will not use your scuba until you are near the platform to preserve your air. All you have to do is unhook the one tank and position it on the well pipe. Magnetic strips on the tank will hold it to the pipe. Then lift the safety latch on the switch and flick the switch. After that, head back to me as fast as you can."

Joe, slack-jawed, murmured, "Hmmmmm."

He was beginning to feel exhilaration well up inside of him. "What an irony. I can get satisfaction and pursue a lifelong dream all at once. Why not? I'm tired of fighting day in and day out, trying to exist because these bastards screwed me. Now I can have it all. Yes, let's do it!"

"We do it tomorrow night."

"Tomorrow night? Isn't that a little fast?"

"There's no time to waste. Deliverance is tomorrow."

"All right! Tomorrow!"

The woman stood up and went to the door. "I'll pick you up at sundown tomorrow night. Do not leave this room for any reason. My people will be watching. Room service is instructed to bring you meals. I will bring the cash tomorrow night as confirmation of our intent."

With a wink and a very provocative look, she said, "You and I will make a great team, don't you think?"

*****

The woman came to the motel the next night right at sundown. Driving the black SUV, she pulled up to Joe's motel room door parking space. The woman took the tote bag with the quarter million dollars into the room, showing Joe the $100 bills inside. Joe was ready but obviously nervous.

"Come on, Joe. Enjoy the moment. This is going to work out well. Destiny is choosing you to play out this drama. It's not everybody who gets the opportunity to get revenge on the ravages of life and rich at the same time. You owe it to yourself!"

"Yes, I know, but somehow, I feel there's something in this I know nothing about. Who's benefiting by this action?"

"Well, for one, you are. Two, I am. You don't think I do this for nothing. And, three, my people get to carry out their plan in affecting the corporate world."

Now Joe seemed to get it. This was industrial sabotage. Well, one corporation preying on the other might level some playing fields by eliminating companies like the bastards that did him in. He was beginning to feel that exhilaration again.

It was dark by the time they got to the dock. They transferred the gear from the SUV to the fishing boat. It was a nice craft. She was fully rigged with depth finders, navigation, radar, and outriggers for trolling. Fishing gear was displayed in all the stowage spots. To anyone watching, it was just another fishing boat that two people were going to sleep in for early morning fishing. Or they might be going out for a romantic evening under the stars. They gathered little notice.

"Joe, you're the fisherman. You've driven this kind of boat before. Take it out. Follow this GPS track and stop at this point. I'm tired." She indicated the track on the instrumentation and then went below.

The drill platform selected by The Committee was one set in fairly deep water. This was to make it more difficult to put out the fire and stop the leak. Located relatively close to land but still far enough out to reach deep water, it was an ideal selection.

It took Joe and his companion an hour and a half to reach the point where Joe would enter the water. It would take him a half hour to snorkel and swim to the platform. Once saddled with all his gear, he slipped into the warm gulf waters. Swimming was Joe's strong suit, and he was conditioned to travel this kind of distance. The water was calm, and the wind was gentle. No chop. So he moved along easily. He could see the drill rig in the distance, and his wrist-mounted GPS told him where he was in relation to the boat and the rig. About twenty minutes out, he stopped using his snorkel and switched to scuba breathing. He dove down about thirty feet and moved to the platform. As he approached the platform, the lights from the rig lit up the water, and Joe could see hundreds of fish of all sizes moving above him.

Wow! Why haven't I fished platforms before? I could have gotten some beauties around these iron works, he thought to himself.

Working his way past the supporting structure, he saw the well pipe descending to the depths. Following it up, he reached the surface. Hoping he was not picked up on any camera from above, he unhitched the tank from his back and placed it on the well pipe.

As Joe was placing the tank on the well pipe, he half expected all hell to break loose as people above might start to descend upon him. But that didn't happen. He suddenly felt as though a great burden was lifted. No longer would he have to be someone else's puppet. He was even.

Reaching up with his finger, he lifted the safety latch on the timer switch. Applying pressure to the switch, he heard the snap as the switch made contact. That was all he heard. In that millisecond, a huge explosion ripped through the steel pipe. Oil and gas under intense pressure spewed and ignited into a giant fireball, enveloping the entire oil platform. In a blink of an eye, Joe was no more.

His companion, watching from the boat, first saw a massive fireball followed by a huge explosion. The shock wave made everything on the boat shudder. Wasting no time, she swung the boat around and disappeared into the night.

CHAPTER 16

Providence

Deliverance proved to be the disaster it was intended to be. Tens of millions of gallons of oil spewed into the ocean, creating oil slicks hundreds of miles long. The environmental damage was huge. Seventeen oil platform workers were killed, with little or no evidence of human remains found. The country was consumed by the incident, and the administration took up their plan of pinning blame. The Committee was satisfied they were able to turn public opinion in their favor once again. There was hope for them in the coming election. As for deliverance? It was considered an accident of monumental proportions due to questionable safety practices and equipment failure. The Committee seemed to have achieved another victory. The force behind the C3P was gathering strength.

Soon, however, an event would take place that would cause many to realize that maybe there was an even greater force in control, a force that interceded without warning.

An energy that was so vast and all-consuming that man had little or no power against it. That when this force would intercede, man's only choice would be to submit to the power of providence and the laws of nature.

The Committee, now in the flush of great socialist and liberal achievements, decided that under the guise of the C3P, it was time to celebrate. Though still a clandestine group, The Committee elected to have a dinner of celebration at their compound in the mountains in late fall. There they would mingle among celebrities, unrecognizable for who they really were, behaving only as guests of the C3P. The intent was to have the president, vice president, speaker of the house, party chairman, and majority leaders present. Additionally, certain members of the C3P, previously selected office holders and major contributors who had supported the ideologies of the C3P, would be all invited to this very exclusive assemblage. Those attending would make their way to the compound in an unobtrusive manner. During the gathering, speeches from selected dignitaries would highlight the event, and food and wine would follow. All in a self-gratification for the many years the C3P had successfully turned the United States of America toward a new order.

The Committee's compound had grown over the years to the size of several thousand acres. The facilities were enhanced somewhat, but the size was due mostly to forested acreage surrounding the compound facilities. A conference center with a large meeting room, offices for The Committee members, and a kitchen were added to accommodate at least one hundred people or more at various selected gatherings. The lake was the centerpiece of the compound, constituting several hundred acres. Over the years, the forest surrounding the compound had become very thick, with lots of dense undergrowth below the towering pines. This created a natural obstacle to intruders even though the compound itself was surrounded by a security fence. Cruising security men would navigate the perimeter of the compound frequently; strategically placed cameras gave on-duty observers a vision of anything trying to access the grounds. The compound was considered by the neighboring population as nothing more than an exclusive hunting lodge for very wealthy people.

Being in the mountains, the compound was located over a fractured bedrock base. Over the eons, seeping from the bowels of the earth and into the fissured layers of rock, methane gas seeped to the surface. Being colorless, odorless, and tasteless, the methane seeped out into the forest and drifted or dissipated into the air, usually carried off by the wind. In recent years, due to minor tremors in the crust of the earth, an increase in fissures allowed for increased amounts of methane gas to reach the surface. Additionally, methane seeping into the bottom of the lake was absorbed into the water because of the cold bottom temperatures and the great pressures at depths of five hundred feet. Water temperatures at the bottom of the lake rarely rose above 40°. At that depth, because of the long cold winters, the lake's bottom temperature seldom moderated much during the few months of summer. Like a bottle of soda water, cold and increased pressure allow carbonation to take place. So too will methane gas dissolve into the water of the lake at cold temperatures and pressure.

Now it so happened that this particular year, the summer had been extremely dry. On top of that, the fall season was now not only dry but also extremely cold. Fall was more like winter, and the trees dropped their leaves rapidly. The forests were like tinderboxes. To add to the hazard, the methane gas seeping up through the earth lay as an invisible pall over the land, held by the dense undergrowth, whenever the air was still.

The lake had absorbed huge amounts of methane gas, especially at the depths. With the fall season being as cold as it was, the lake started to freeze around the edges, and the surface temperatures were beginning to reach colder temperatures than the lake bottom. This would mean that the lake would go through a phenomenon whereby the lake would "turn over," that is, the bottom waters would roll upward and the surface waters would sink because of their increased density. This upwelling would cause a change, aiding events that would seem impossible.

The evening of The Committee's special gathering arrived with all the expectations that the ideologues hoped to see and hear. The guests came in scattered groups by individual car or limousine. Some were obviously accompanied by Secret Service personnel or bodyguards. Others came alone or with the company of a companion. To get into the compound, all had been given a special pass that was inspected at the perimeter gate entrance to the compound. It, along with all invited personnel, was verified once again when their vehicle arrived at the inner compound facility.

The compound facility was separated from the compound perimeter by a distance of two miles through the forest. There was only one road in and the same road out for security reasons.

As everyone arrived, the invited group assembled in the meeting room of the compound that was organized in seating arrangements that imitated a large reception. A head table at the front of the hall was set for special dignitaries or speakers, and the remainder of the hall was set up with round tables for seating and dining. Special bars were placed for the dispersal of cocktails, beer, and wine. Everybody moved about before the great dinner, mingling throughout the hall, acquainting themselves with all the guests, inquiring as to who was who and what was what, and reminiscing with one another on past accomplishments. Eventually, speakers made their presentations, congratulatory orations were made, and the evening turned into music, dancing, and revelry.

The final main speaker of the evening was the president. Introduced by the C3P party chairman, he ambled up to the dais, looking confident with a hint of cockiness. To a roar of acceptance, he addressed the group. "Today, I stand before you, knowing we have made a difference. This country today is not the same country we knew forty years ago. Our accomplishments have been significant, and we have made this nation ours. I congratulate all of you in making this happen. Now! Enough talk, let's have a good time."

Again, there was a roar and ovation, and everyone went about enjoying themselves.

Coincidently with all the activity, The Committee members were moving among the guests, taking up conversations of chitchats or serious topics. Every so often, someone would come up to Ivan and say, "Who do you suppose The Committee members are? Do you think they're here tonight?"

Ivan would simply smile and say, "I doubt it. I think they would just as soon stay anonymous."

One such curious guest had to pursue it. "Yeah, you're probably right. It sure makes them a mysterious group, though. By the way, what's your part in all this? I don't remember seeing you before."

It was easy for Ivan to respond. "Oh, I'm not from this part of the country. I usually am involved on the fundraising side, and as you might expect, it takes me all over the globe. I got an invitation to this gathering, and luckily, I was in the area to be able to come."

"Fundraising, huh? You must have made a big difference to get invited with this prestigious group."

Now it was starting to get too personal, so Ivan excused himself and moved on.

Casper also mingled. Merlin's description of Casper as a pip-squeak fit him to a T; much older now, he was more curmudgeon than pip-squeak and walked with a cane. People didn't readily draw themselves to him since he avoided getting into conversations. Although one person did stop him to ask, "You remind me of a person I saw on a TV program many years ago. I don't remember his name, but you look just like him. You wouldn't be him, would you?"

The person was "half in the bag," so Casper simply ignored him.

Merlin easily moved about the assemblage. Drink in one hand and the other hand gesturing as he talked with some attractive wife of one of the guests, he appeared to be more of a very old Don Juan than a political ideologue. It would hardly occur to anyone that he was a member of The Committee.

Juno had aged very well. Still slim, she had also retained her vigor and mental acuity. She sought out those who had more of her bent for financial or economic discussion. Naturally, these conversations took up the subject of where money for the party would come from and how it should be distributed, boring stuff to most who were there to have a good time.

The only embarrassing part of the evening was when the vice president, who had started drinking before he arrived, reached the loud and boisterous stage. For some reason, he started ranting about being relegated to a figurehead status in the administration.

Slurring his words, he said, "All I do is stand on my two feet and act the statesman. Nobody wants me to do anything but look the part. No decisions, no action, and when I try to say something, I'm told to keep quiet and mind my matters-er-manners. It's not right. I don't like it, and you're all against me."

His wife, obviously irritated and embarrassed, asked for help to get him to a side room. A couple of attendants helped convince him to go with her.

As the hours went on, more and more of the guests were feeling the effects of serious drinking.

While this grand celebration was taking place, a chain of events began to unfold in a most eerie and implausible way. To begin with, the night was absolutely still and cold. The methane gas that seeped out of the ground had for days been building up in the understory of the forest, and tonight, like an invisible blanket, it drifted throughout the forest compound. Next, at the entrance to the compound, through pure circumstance, a tree's rotted limb broke loose under its weight and fell upon power lines stretched across the entrance road. With a great flash, sparks showered down to the forest floor at the entry/exit point to the compound. The tinder-dry forest matter burst into flame instantly. The fire blazed outward and upward.

As the forest suddenly burst into flame at the compounds entrance, fire and security alarms blared as the guests were in the height of frivolity. Not understanding what was happening, many immediately went outside and saw a brightness of light that seemingly moved toward and, at the same time, around them. Something seemed to have sucked the oxygen out of the air, and in no time, the guests could see and feel flames descend upon them.

The unimaginable had happened. Like fuming gasoline, the methane gas envelope that hung in the forest flashed over at an incredible speed. Rushing through the entire forest compound, everything ignited into curtains of flame. Within minutes, the entire forest compound was an inferno from one end to the other. There was no time for anyone to react. The fire erupted with such enormity that escape was impossible. The entire forest compound now ablaze caused a driving inward rush of wind that provided oxygen like a gigantic blacksmith's forge, escalating heat to thousands of degrees. The howl of the entire forest in flame was as deafening as hundreds of jet engines.

As though the firestorm wasn't enough, the lake that always looked beautiful and serene was now about to add an even more improbable and catastrophic addition to this chain of events. The lake, like a giant punch bowl, did its roll over. As the water from the depths began to surge upward, the methane gas dissolved within began to come out of solution and effervesce. The surface of the lake started to fizz as the methane gas was released into the air. Instantly, as the gas rose into the air, it ignited, making it appear as though the lake was actually burning. As the superheat of the surrounding forest fire combined with the ignited gas over the lake, the surface temperature of the lake rose, causing the gas to bubble up even faster. The whole combination created a firestorm of such massive proportions that everything faced complete annihilation.

A tornado of flame whirled over a thousand feet into the air. Plants, animals, insects, serpents, and man were incinerated on the spot in most cases, not slowly but abruptly, bursting into flames and then disappearing as the intense heat vaporized all. Remains of any living thing were eradicated, bearing only ash or momentary vapor with no evidence as to whom or what was there. Wire oxidized into granules of grit and metals melted into pools. Even glass melted into swirls of what later looked like remains of a large, melted candle. Buildings of the compound would burst into flame and then vaporize or turn into ash and dust. Automobiles burned out completely, their component parts consumed, then melting into puddles of liquid metal. Concrete structures crumbled under the intense heat, merging with the ground as so much rubble. Nothing or anyone escaped the complete eradication of what were once people, places, and things of this giant compound in the mountains. The fire burned so completely and so quickly that soon the fire used up its fuel and burned itself out. With the exception of incidental fires that burned beyond the perimeter of the compound, the maelstrom of fire and destruction came to an end.

Local authorities, aware of the huge conflagration that just played itself out in their domain, found them struggling to understand why such an event occurred? Walking the area, the earth under them crunched. The sand had fused together into a layer of glass from the intense heat and now fractured like ice on a frozen puddle as they walked through this barren prairie of destruction. They were awestruck as they looked upon several thousand acres of land now devoid of anything. A snow-white ash lay upon the ground, and pools of hardened metal and glass reflected in the sunlight. As a breeze played across the landscape, dust devils of white ash lifted upward into the sky like escaping spirits anxious to leave this desolation. A surreal vision of nothingness lay before them.

CHAPTER 17

The Aftermath

Who would have ever expected that in a period of one day, so many important high government office holders would be wiped off the face of the earth? The nation was in a crisis. The president and all his successors had vanished, down through the secretary of the Treasury. The heir apparent was now the secretary of defense. Even below his position, cabinet members had disappeared because of this catastrophe.

The C3P, having lost its guiding force, was thrown into complete disarray. The Committee, so long the power behind the party, was gone. Those who wanted to carry on the ideology of a nation became like gangs in the underworld. When the leadership is eliminated, the lackeys are lost in the confusion. Some want to cut out a place for themselves while others form devious partnerships with outsiders. There is no honor among thieves. And, for those who wanted to abandon the notions of the past, they were at a loss as to where to begin.

The Senate moved quickly to empower the new president so leadership would be quickly established. Politics was finally set aside by both parties for the sake of unity and bipartisanship to put the pieces back together. Every effort had to be made to prevent foreign nations from exercising ill intent or allowing them to take advantage of the current state of affairs. A new president whose experience in military applications and an inherent understanding of the foreign threats worldwide made for a fortuitous transition. Immediately, the president put the military on alert throughout the whole world. He raised the nation's homeland security alert to the highest level. To replace the vacancies that now existed in this void of leadership, much were needed to be done.

While the leadership of both parties in the House and Senate were working to reestablish the structures of government in the face of national calamity, it was determined that an investigation must take place to understand what happened. Why were so many key office holders united in such a disaster? Congress quickly established an investigative panel to seek out answers.

The president, left with a nation in turmoil, sought out those individuals who might have some insight as to how so many people of national importance were together and then snuffed out at this seemingly remote and now barren location.

The new CIA director, meeting with the president, briefed him on the existence of the Articles of Acquisition.

The director said, "Mr. President, you should know that there was also a committee that was the force behind the C3P. I say was because we believe it no longer exists. I would like to introduce you to a man who has some knowledge about this situation, and he was involved early on."

"Who is this person?"

"His name is Jim Cooper, an older retired FBI agent who suspected early on that there was a conspiracy of sorts and has knowledge of the goings on in the C3P. He revealed his concerns to an earlier president while he was working in the White House."

"Well, bring him on! I need to know what he knows!"

Jim Cooper was summoned to the White House. As he approached the great office of the president, he wondered what the new world was going to bring. After tumultuous years of great divisions in the thinking of the country, the polarization of political entities, to the right and to the left, the seemingly relentless rush to a socialized nation, all of it now seemed to promise an end. But—what kind of end? Would we flounder as a confused and troubled nation? Or would the life of this country, once again, move forward into the broad sunlit uplands of individual freedom and prosperity?

The CIA director introduced Jim Cooper at the door of the Oval Office to the president of the United States. The president, standing in the doorway, looked as though he had already aged ten years. Taking Jim by the arm and walking him into the great room, the door closed behind them.

The nation was thrust into a vacuum of political discipline; the two parties struggled to find meaning in the seemingly Armageddon events that took place. To the general population, those who had a deep-seeded faith looked upon the tragedy as recompense by Almighty God for the devious acts that were taking place throughout the nation as instituted by the C3P and the so called Committee. Less spiritually influenced citizens looked upon it as a natural disaster, no more, no less. Yet, even among these skeptics, there was a fragment of belief that something powerful had wiped out a movement that was not intended to exist since this force erased the elements of its existence so completely.

Throughout the country, the elements of the C3P now tried to hold on to the precepts The Committee had instituted. Due to a lack of meaningful leadership, there was more chaos than organized direction. Animosity and radical behavior began to dominate the C3P. Disruption and descent into an anarchy form of protest began to wind through elements of the party all over the nation. Soon flagrant actions of violence popped up from outside groups, invading certain cities where liberal governance was allowing penetration of these forces. The nation had evolved from a poor, middle-class, upper-class structure into a four-tiered society. The legitimately poor class, the indolent parasitic class, a traditional working middle class, and the well-to-do.

The president, finishing out the remnant term of office he inherited, had no intention of running for election. His forte was the military. He served the office well, but he was out of his element. The C3P, left void of meaningful candidates, chose nominees as close to their intended objective of a socialist state as they could find. No matter, the country had its fill of radical behavior and put its hope in a new and different kind of president. The new president won easily, and his first act in office was to expose the Articles of Acquisition promulgated by the now defunct Committee. The crass and overt meanings in the thirteen articles so enraged the population that a great unity of purpose to return to the freedoms the founders of our nation had implemented became a rallying cry. The administration, seeing the popular revulsion of what the nation saw as treasonous acts to implement a new order, immediately called for an investigating committee to find and prosecute anyone suspected of contributing to or participating in treasonous activity associated with the past.

The C3P, complicit in its actions of the past, shrunk into a shadow of itself, and a new party emerged with the intention of providing the nation with a new vision of freedom and mutual cooperation. Its purpose was to see to the unity of mankind based on the principles of faith and cooperative understanding. A party by the people, not for the sake of power, but for the purpose of peace and harmony. Moved by patriotism and guided by God's truth, it would lead the country into the freedom and prosperity of those broad sunlit uplands so often promised.

ARTICLES OF ACQUISITION

Article 1: The end will justify the means whether or not traditionally amoral or immoral.

Article 2: The growing civil rights movement will be exploited for the party's own sake and not necessarily for the best interest of minorities or underprivileged. As a fact of history, give them what they can get for little or nothing, and they will obligate themselves to you. The general population will then support the party because Americans love the underdog.

Article 3: The growing feminist movement must be exploited. By supporting them, it will foster planned parenthood and abortion. By furthering a general acceptance among the population, it will diminish the need for family unity and further the goal of government involvement in child welfare and population control.

Article 4: Exploit the liberal establishment and their ideals. By promoting liberal attitudes, the general degradation of traditional moral concepts will pave the way for socialist involvement through government intervention.

Article 5: Debase the religious right and particularly the Catholic Church. Socialism has no place for religion.

Article 6: Support gun control in all its forms. By placing weapons only in the hands of government authorities, government strengthens its dominance over the citizenry.

Article 7: Support the unions, particularly the corrupt and mafia-influenced unions. They will become the enforcers in our new society. When all government agencies and all associated government departments are unionized, they will become the shakers and movers to bend the general population to the governments will.

Article 8: Infiltrate the biggest businesses in the land. Seek out the corrupt and encourage them to exploit these companies to the point where government must take them over. Start with the banks and mortgage lenders, then the key industrial corporations.

Article 9: Education is to be dominated by liberal educators so as to allow indoctrination of the tenets of a socialist system into the minds of our young people. It must start at government-controlled preschools and through the high schools. Colleges and universities that support liberal thinking should be encouraged so as to develop within the minds of their students socialist ideals. The liberal colleges, universities, and institutions should be the source of advisors, drawn from the academic staff, to mentor our bureaucratic and political planners.

Article 10: The media, as predominantly liberal, should be exploited so as to encourage biased reporting in all its forms. Through its vast reporting capability, it will act as a conciliatory voice to our cause and bring constant criticism to our adversaries. They have the power to turn the thinking of the population in our direction.

Article 11: The entertainment industry, long a liberal and amoral industry, must be encouraged to liberalize and further debase the population. By their degradation of family and family values and by fostering sexual freedom in all its forms, they will make it easier to establish socialist controls when and where we want.

Article 12: Taxation should be maximized wherever and whenever possible as a matter of course. By creating a complex tax burden, the government always has the upper hand in assessing and spending. Since the bureaucrats and politicians control the use of funds, they can enrich themselves at the expense of the population and remain the elite.

Article 13: The environmentalists must be exploited by encouraging them to exaggerate the effects of mankind on nature. By continually expounding on man's responsibility for the effects taking place with the changes in the environment, mankind takes the position that government is the only answer to man's destiny. Vast financial sums will be directed toward typically liberal environmental establishments who can then be persuaded to direct some of those resources to our cause.

PART 2

A Cataclysmic Event

INTRODUCTION
TO PART TWO

In Part One the hand of Providence dealt a destructive force that emaciated a political entity bent on establishing a *new order*. This supposed *new order* was based on principles devised in a demonic way that would convert the United States of America to a socialist state. Godless in its intent, it had brought destruction upon itself, but not completely. Born of free enterprise and a capitalist system, certain creative individuals built technical and space-age empires that blossomed into worldwide influence.

These individuals became billionaires and drunk with their successes; they decided to form an elite group once again with the intent of dominating the nation and even the world. It was their intent to unite with the social and mainstream media moguls, and together they would accomplish a means to unify the population under the mantel of total allegiance to a new elitist class. Abiding by the principles of the *Articles of Acquisition*, which established the precepts to achieve socialism, they now added their own flavor to the mixture. Technology would now control all aspects of life, and the media would propagandize and censor through false information and intimidation. Space exploitation would also be used to control the earth from above.

The hierarchy of the C3P (Citizens' Progressive Populist Party), though vanishing from the face of the earth, had left its mark on the remnants of party loyalists. These loyalists were intent on moving their ideology ahead no matter the aftermath of the disastrous events that wiped out every segment of leadership within their party. Like a phoenix rising from the ashes of devastation, a new cadre of idealists, intent on pursuing extremist domination in the United States and even to the ends of the earth, formed a new cabal to destroy the ATP (American Traditional Party) now in power and to direct its will upon the people once again.

Now, however, they would be dealing with a new movement forged within the ATP to bring about a third party—a party of lofty ideals to bring a peaceful unity to the nation, based on the intentions of the founders, but supplemented with a code of ethics that transcended all previous parties. This code of ethics became the antithesis of the *Articles of Acquisition*. It was established as the *Articles of Reconciliation*. Designed to unify the nation under the protection of the constitution and to establish a brotherhood between all peoples and free-loving nations.

CHAPTER 1

A Bold Beginning

After the C3P hierarchy was wiped out by the conflagration in their forest compound, the party lost its place in the hearts of the American people. At the next election, the ATP won handily, and the new president began to establish new life into what was a lackluster state of American prosperity and morale. Besides, like the unions, the two parties started off as organizations dedicated to looking out for the best interests of the people, but over time, instead of servants of the people, they began to operate to bring about more power to the party. The party and its leadership were the intended benefactors, not the people.

Daniel Solomon was as wise as he was cunning. A wealthy man in his own right, he aspired to the office of President because strongly anti-elitist and recognizing the rights of every individual to succeed on their individual merits, he detested what the C3P had as their ideology. President Solomon did not mince words, spoke his mind, intimidated anyone who spoke action, and did nothing. He wasn't always liked, but he gained respect by his *get-it-done* efforts. He had no sympathy for ATP politicians who built their career on winning elections without doing anything meaningful during their terms in office, especially those entrenched long-termed individuals who feathered their beds but did nothing for their constituency or the nation. And since the preponderance of ATP politicians now in office came under this latter political description, it appeared that only a new party with a higher set of principles would have to be inaugurated. This party would have to begin now as a branch of the ATP, quiet in its development and steadfast in its intent.

For the present, however, it was time to get things done to reverse the forces of evil brought about by C3P. They had implemented so much in the way of socialist, liberal policies that the nation was suffering from hatred, complacency, stagnation, and government dependency. It was truly a polarized country—traditional, conservative, hard-working, faithful, and loving on one side; liberal, indolent, permissive, licentious, greedy, and godless on the other.

After reversing, by executive order, several of the previous executive orders initiated by the C3P's POTUS, President Solomon set about solidifying his cohort of operatives in the current administration. Through his actions, optimism began to take hold throughout the country. Jobs and the economy picked up steam. Everything was on the upswing, and it looked as though the country would work its way out of the doldrums of lackluster performance as a nation and bring sunshine and promise once again. But that was not to be.

Through intimidation, direct and deliberate distortion of the truth, the new cabal of the C3P attacked President Solomon and all of the ATP operatives in office. Their use of the mainstream and social media to obfuscate, distort, and vilify every move the administration made served to place doubt into the population's impression of President Solomon and his current administration. Hatred was the byword, and every means of expression was used, including obscene language and abusive rhetoric as never before. Try as they may, the ATP was hard put to fend off criticism. The power of the tech giant communication entities and the mainstream media pounded out their flood of hatred in massive proportions. The only thing the ATP could do was to remain steadfast in their objectives. From this, a new code of ethics began to form. The *Articles of Reconciliation* was now to be formulated.

It was obvious that to accomplish all the new objectives and to convince the country that only a new party was the answer, much work had to be done. Only by a manipulative path of secret negotiations among like-minded individuals would a plan to replace an old, entrenched party by a new party be possible. But the plan had to include a means of swaying the public to accepting the new party. New parties have never succeeded in gaining acceptable popularity sufficient to hold any kind of sway in the country. To succeed, something different had to be done to gain acceptance by a large segment of the nation.

CHAPTER 2

A New Administration

Despite overwhelming odds, the ATP had managed to implement many positive changes that saw the economy flourish, the unemployment evaporated through every segment of the country, and the general well-being of the majority of individuals proved to improve their lot. However, the misinformation, deliberate obfuscation, and smear campaigns across the country coupled with grave doubts as to the legitimacy of vote counts proved too much. The C3P was back in power. Whether legitimately or illegitimately, it remained a mystery since the justice department and SCOTUS did not respond to charges of voter fraud. During the eight years of C3P dominance prior to the now-passing administration, the justice department, including the FBI, was compromised by socialist influence. The C3P influence on the entire bureaucracy was tainted by that administration. On top of that, as though a sign had been put on the country for all to see, a pandemic of world proportions stifled everything the ATP set out to do, including members of their own party working against itself.

Now the C3P managed to get their new president in office. Too old to think rationally and with a load of baggage involving family scandals, the new president displayed ambiguity, dementia, and incoherent ramblings. This came to a head when at a speech at the Arlington National Cemetery, the new president began to rant (off script) by not only criticizing the size of the military, but he said that he was ready to eliminate 50 percent of all service-related activity, not only at home but also abroad. This shook up the nation so badly that the C3P was forced to contrive a story that somehow his medication had been overprescribed and he had to be hospitalized a few days to regulate his condition back to normal. He was immediately hospitalized, and his handlers see to it that he would stay out of the limelight as much as possible. Instead, his vice president would stand in for him, and his press secretary would handle any White House press conferences. It looked as though his aides were going to run the country at the direction of the tech and media moguls who had formed their own *committee*.

The new *committee* decided to refer to themselves as *The Committee* as well, since they were picking up where the old *committee* had left off. This *committee*, however, had a bolder and more all-encompassing plan. Their plan was a world controlled by a few through a worldwide technical exchange. That exchange would be run by a few to master the many with the latest technology. They would see to it that the population would become totally dependent on technology to carry out their daily life. It would no longer be necessary for the general population to be educated in a classroom as long as they had the necessary devices to make any decisions. This was looked upon as a means of purging all people of independent thought and making them slaves to their technological devices and therefore to their tech-masters. *The Committee* would implement governmental, social, and industrial management according to engineers and administer through technologists. They would soon call the party the *Technocratic Progressive Party* or T2P for short. In their view, technology would be god; the technologists would be the angels to manage electronically controlled consciences, and the devil would be anybody who defied the omniscience of technological advancement.

The Committee began to reform the government through an orientation of the civil service and political bureaucrats that amounted to *brainwashing*. Demanding strict obedience to the dictates of *The Committee*, the bureaucrats knew they had to comply because there were too many stories of missing fellow department managers who had failed to heed the precepts of the *Articles of Acquisition* that still was the code of the party. *The Committee* set about to establish a new compound for their clandestine meetings. They managed to acquire a large piece of land that happened to be a mountain in the Rockies.

Too high to have undergrowth, there were no worries about conflagrations. The mountain was hollowed out to create a large cavern to place the massive electronic storage devices consisting of supercomputers to watch everything and everybody. However, the mountain was to be a facade. It was referred to as a nuclear waste disposal storage area, leased to the government and secured twenty-four hours a day to prevent exposure to alleged radiation. It would also be the headquarters of *The Committee*. It was a perfect place to operate a worldwide technocratic empire, led by megalomaniacs drunk with the power of their wealth and influence.

With the space tech moguls secretly placing satellites around the globe, no one was safe from prying eyes in the sky. Control rooms in the mountain would be managed by tech gurus, who would convey information to the leadership or through the media entities that made up part of *The Committee*; propaganda and disinformation could be disseminated. In other words, every phone, computer, and electronic-computing device in the public domain would be hacked, and every detail of every individual would be known to the supercomputer. The supercomputer known as *Cyclops* was to be one eye that sees everything. It would seem that *The Committee* was creating a pagan idol to be worshipped and obeyed.

The chairman of *The Committee*, one of the billionaire creators of one of the original desktop computers, took on the name of *Zeus*. This was in keeping with the mythology theme associated with the supercomputer. Like as his name implied, *Zeus* was god of lightning and would be the motivator in establishing a new technological order for the implementation of a totalitarian existence among the nations of the world.

At one of *The Committee's* first meetings, Zeus introduced the fact that the president was a real threat to the party. Poorly chosen as a nominee to begin with, it was too late to do anything now that he was firmly in office. But to solve the problem, something had to be done. *The Committee* was queried as to suggestions as to how to negate the problem. At this juncture, one of the members who was, in his own right, a master engineer in the field of simulation and animation and robotics suggested that through his technicians, he could come up with a solution.

It was offered for consideration that through presenting the president to the public as a perfect likeness in the form of an android, they could present the president as hale, compassionate, charismatic, alert, and above all, stable.

Zeus immediately asked the question, "How do you expect to do this?"

The master engineer responded by saying, "We have the capability through advanced robotic technology, 3D digital scanning and 3D printing using skin-like polymer materials to form a human android to replace our human president and make him look and sound like one of the most capable presidents that we have ever had. We can simulate his mouth, voice sound, and lip and facial action and sync it with an off-camera individual who will be scripted for every statement or speech he will make.

"In other words, we will have an android president who we will completely control any time we need to put him before the public. By keeping our real president in essentially posh solitary confinement, we don't ever have to expose him as a real person. In fact, if we can find a close double and touch him up cosmetically, we can use him at public appearances or signing ceremonies, as long as he is controlled by his handlers and is limited in his presence."

Zeus liked the idea and so did the rest of *The Committee*. Immediate action was taken to carry out all that was necessary to create an *android president*.

CHAPTER 3

Island in the Sun

Former ATP President Solomon, out of office and anxious to form a party that would be united to its people, called together select members of the ATP as well as associates from the private sector to formulate a plan to reestablish *one nation under God with liberty and justice for all.*

The only way that Daniel Solomon could see the ability to plan a means of creating a new party under extreme secrecy was to find an island away from mainland USA and assemble his group there to headquarter their organization. Having the financial means to purchase an island, he acquired the island through an old acquaintance who gladly sold him the island he had owned for many years. Anonymity was understood by all concerned. The island, though exposed to hurricanes during the summer, was still the best location. Set in the Caribbean, it was the perfect place, with its own slips for boats and a private airstrip for private planes or helicopters. The facility had all the essentials to function independently from a mainland. Security was easily established to protect it from intruders as it functioned as a private estate. The most secure means of traveling to and from the island was by boat, where electronic-tracking devices could be turned off. Set up as a sleep on fishing yacht, movement would gain little notice.

Daniel Solomon chose five associates to join his planning group. Each one was strong in their respective fields of knowledge. It's not important to elaborate on their specialties or who did what in the way of action. As a cohesive group, their interactions proved the means to getting things done. Since they were all doers, things could be accomplished on a reliable basis. The first thing was to determine a starting point.

Daniel assumed the lead position and served as the presider on all planning. So at their first meeting on the island compound, all assembled to get the ball rolling.

Daniel said, "Well, how do we get started. You all know what our intent is. The tough part is where do we begin?"

Joanna was the president's former press secretary. Her broad experience in public relations and communications gave her the expertise needed in communicating with the public. She knew how to handle any necessity for broad exposure to the public, and she was the first to speak.

"I believe that we need to develop a vast network of individuals across the nation who will be of our mindset and use them to stimulate their area of responsibility. This stimulation must be a campaign of communicating an undercurrent of thinking among the population, through the use of an *Articles of Reconciliation*. It should be our immediate goal to establish these *articles* and then proceed to convey our intent through our network. I've begun a start to these *articles*, and now we as a group should complete them according to the principles we all desire."

Daniel agreed, "There's no time like the present, so let's get started. Joanna, start us off."

Joanna viewed her notes and then began, "To begin with, I believe we should start with the fundamental basis for our existence. It should be the intent of the party to apply all action according to a God-based moral standard. We all know what that standard is since it has held true ever since Moses came down from that mountain. I offer this as Article I. So starting with Article I: 'It is the intent of the party to apply all action according to a God-based moral standard.'"

The group proceeded to establish seventeen articles. It became the group's guiding force for the conveyance of an intent of reconciliation to all citizens.

After the *articles* were established, Daniel exhorted the group to determine the individuals who would incorporate the dissemination of the new movement's intent. This was to be done expeditiously, and they would meet again every day during the week to see how everyone was developing their effort.

In the meantime, Daniel had selected a former intelligence officer to be part of the group. He had been highly placed as national intelligence director during Daniel's administration. A true patriot and supporter of all the principles of the *Articles of Reconciliation*, he was knowledgeable in all aspects of security and knew the ins and outs as well as the most trustworthy individuals in the intelligence community. Daniel made it clear to him that he knew that based on subliminal information the C3P was up to something directed toward people control and technological advancement. It was Daniel's desire when he said, "We have to somehow penetrate the means to find out the C3P's intent. When we do, if we can't expose them for what they are, this country will be in deep trouble. So, John Brooks, I'm requesting that you begin the process of finding out what is going on in the C3P camp."

At this point, Daniel, Joanna, and John, three of the six operatives, activated to begin the ball rolling. Now it remains to get the remaining three members out and about, implementing through contacts, an awakening, as it were, of the conscience of the people.

It was determined that of the three remaining members, they would be assigned areas in three sections. The east to the Mississippi River, the middle from the Mississippi to the Rockies, and the west to the Pacific Ocean. Whatever they needed to do to develop a cadre of lieutenants to assist them in their efforts, they would be trusted to do. Just get the job done.

As far as this group was concerned, only Daniel, Joanna, and John would go by their names. The other three would be known as Echo, Mike, and Whiskey, each first letter representing their territory of responsibility.

CHAPTER 4

A Secret Enclave

The Group, as they called themselves, began to work out the necessities to inform the public, through personal network connections. Still involved with the ATP, their intent was to eventually create their own party based on the precepts of the *Articles of Reconciliation*. To some, they might be looked at as conspirers, but to themselves, they looked upon themselves as saviors of a nation. The ATP was not living up to its original intentions, and old-line members did not intend to change their ways. The C3P was a threat to the country, and *The Group* did not intend to let this happen.

Having set in motion a chain of events, *The Group* set about to accomplish their goals. The first was to find out what the C3P was up to.

Acting per the authority of Daniel, John began to seek out those in the intelligence community he could trust to give him information. Many in the various intelligence services were very concerned about what was taking place under the current administration, known only by the signs of influence that was coming to bear on each department.

John's first contact was to be one of his former assistants who was still a holdover from when John was director of national intelligence. John felt that it would be best to approach him as if he was just looking to see how old friends were doing, meet him for lunch at some quiet out-of-the-way restaurant, and see what information his old assistant might volunteer.

So on one bright sunny day, John called his old working partner in Washington DC and arranged for a luncheon meeting, just to get caught up on each other's personal life. They met at a country restaurant outside of town.

John's old assistant was known as *Whisper*, because he was soft-spoken. What he lacked in strength of voice, he made up for in physique and stature. A very impressive gentleman whose bearing was unmistakable—honest to the core and very reliable. He would be a great asset in sourcing information. But he had to be convinced before he would commit to anything. That was going to be the hard part, but John would worry about that later.

Sitting down at a remote corner table in the restaurant, John asked Whisper how things were going. He noticed that Whisper was not his old self. He seemed preoccupied in a way. Whisper responded, "Oh, I've been all right. The family is good, everybody is healthy, and the kids are now in college. My only concern these days is what is this country coming to."

That was all that John needed to hear. He found the soft spot he was looking for and now just needed to figure out on how to exploit the opportunity.

John responded, "Yes, I'm concerned in a major way. Being essentially retired, I don't have to be in the midst of it as you are. I don't have to deal with the political pressures, and I can tell you that's a big relief."

Whisper rolled his eyes, and knowing his position in government bound him to secrecy, he could only nod his head or acknowledge with an approving glance. Perhaps though, without revealing specifics, he could allude to strange happenings he has not been let in on at the department level. So he suggested to John that they plan a golf game where they could talk freely. And that's what they did. A week later, they were on a golf course together taking in a round of golf.

John got into his approach to seeing what Whisper would discuss by opening up a conversation about himself. "I've been staying pretty busy. I'm working with some very interesting people who are also worried about our country's future but are looking to figure out a way to get things right again." Whisper's interest was evident. John continued, "The thing that has got us really worried is that the tech industry, and the media moguls seem to be teaming up to control everything."

At that, Whisper said, "Yes, I don't think I'm revealing any secrets, since I haven't been briefed on the subject, but recently, the GSA signed a lease on a property in the Rockies. It's a mountain, and supposedly, it is being hollowed out as a nuclear waste site. Funny thing though, for some reason, a lot of tech engineers and space vehicle sub-contractors are involved. The media doesn't seem to take an interest, so there's no publicity surrounding it. There's more here than meets the eye."

Aha! This is just what John was looking for. He now has something to zero in on. He said to Whisper, "If you learn more on this, I certainly would be interested in knowing what you hear through the grapevine. I think something stinky is going on."

At the next meeting of *The Group*, John conveyed to everyone Whisper's revelation. It was determined by all present that somehow they had to find out what really was going on. They had to get more information.

In the meantime, Echo, Mike, and Whiskey had contacted several lead individuals in their respective territories to organize in cities and towns, groups who would rally support for a new movement. They targeted church groups, conservative organizations, conservative radio-talking heads, young people's anti-liberal groups, military retirees, and supporters of patriotic tradition. They then presented them with the new movement's *Articles of Reconciliation* as a covenant between the new movement and the people.

All who united with the new movement were pledged to its objective, the reversal of what was going on in government. Over the next two years, not only did the new movement take hold, particularly in rural America, but also in the periphery of the big cities. The big cities were so dependent on federal help to prop them up, and the city populace was becoming so agnostic in their thinking that being led by a central power was attractive to their desires.

It didn't look as though the new movement was going to have a big impact on big city dwellers.

Like Babel and Sodom and Gomorrah, the big cities were becoming vile centers of corruption, greed, licentiousness, and pagan in their desire for all thing's material. Sadly, they constituted a very large segment of the voting population and coupled with outlying centers of such liberality. It looked unlikely that any new movement would have the ability to win by democratic means any majority position to make a difference. Despite this adversity, they would press on as best as they could. Perhaps, Providence would take a hand once again.

CHAPTER 5

A Virtual President

During the first two years in office, the president was confined to his posh solitary confinement in a safe house protected by his handlers. The technology gurus had done such a complete job of virtualizing the president that his existence was considered no different than a real person occupying office. At the same time, the C3P was finishing their center of operations in the Rocky Mountains. Supercomputers had been installed, and the digestion of information on every individual in the United States was being stored in the memory banks of Cyclops, the all-seeing eye for the power that now ran the country. It was only a matter of time before it was fully operational to carry out the process of complete domination of mind, body, and soul of the citizens of the nation. Technology would be the dictator of all thought through the man-made devices people were now completely depending upon. The power behind the technology was *The Committee*.

As it happens, the real president, though thinking he was running the country, was only living an imaginary life produced by his handlers. They did a good job of it until one day he overheard two individuals discussing the subject. They had commented by saying, "If he only knew what was going on."

By now, his dementia had advanced to the point to where he had a hard time remembering most things. His days were mostly a blur, and he was becoming more and more depressed. He became paranoid to the point of suspecting that everybody was scheming against him. Finally, *The Committee* viewed him as dangerous and abiding by their *articles*, determined it was necessary for him to be permanently neutralized. His handlers prepared the necessary means for the president to commit suicide, and it all occurred quietly. In the meantime, the virtual president continued to run the country via *The Committee*. Only the immediate family knew of his passing, and they weren't going to say anything, acting as though everything was going as normal. This was to continue for the remaining two years of the president's term in office. Unless, something happened to change all that.

Zeus confronted *The Committee* by saying, "We have resolved one problem, but we have another. The president's family is a threat. We need to now find a way to eliminate the whole family because they are in a position to blackmail us. Knowing their background, they are not to be trusted. Too much is at stake."

So *The Committee* elected one of their agents to organize an accident that would take out the whole family, all at once, exclusive of the president who was no longer a threat since he was eliminated earlier.

The agent's name was Cosmo. He concluded that the best way to eliminate the family would be by an air accident. He would lure the family by creating a false opportunity by a foreign country that would offer the family a multimillion-dollar opportunity they couldn't resist. Since the family was corrupted early on by money, what better way than to lure them into another scheme. So the first step was to determine what country and what the enticement would be. Then it was just a matter of getting them on a plane and sending them to their inevitable end.

Through an anonymous source, the prime minister of a former Soviet bloc nation was contacted with an offer from presumably the son of the president of the United States. Actually it was a dubbed phone call. The pseudo son suggested that through his influence, he would be able to steer his country toward doing business with the prime minister. The prime minister was as corrupt as the president's son and agreed to the meeting. It was made clear that the deal was worth five hundred million dollars, and the son and his family wanted an *in-person* meeting with him to talk of terms.

Simultaneously, the agent contacted the deceased president's son, and by dubbing the prime minister's voice, the prime minister offered a 20 percent share in a five-hundred-million-dollar deal if he and his family would come to his country to work out the terms of the deal. Since both parties agreed, *The Committee* see to it that the necessary arrangements were made and that the media would keep the trip secret. Cosmo then arranged for a private jet to carry the family to the intended country. Except there was one wrinkle. Cosmo see to it that the oxygen tanks on board the aircraft were nonfunctional. Once the plane was at altitude requiring oxygen, the lack of oxygen would immediately render all on board unconscious. By then, the plane would be on automatic pilot and would be on a doctored course across the ocean, flying until it ran out of fuel, falling into the ocean, never to be found.

The family left Washington, DC, on its way to a rendezvous from which they would never return. The official pronouncement was that the family had chartered a plane to go to an unnamed Caribbean Island for a vacation when some tragic event must have occurred with the plane. Since the flight plan that was filed didn't match with the actual flight of the plane, it was determined that an avionics malfunction or an onboard mechanical failure occurred. The NTSB had nothing to go on to determine what happened, and though the case was left open, no further action took place. *The Committee* see to it that the virtual president, bereft in his appearance, made the announcement to the nation.

During the remainder of the C3P President in office, *The Committee* would make great strides in completing the mountain center of technological control that was to be used to manipulate the entire population. Another two years, and they should have absolute mastery over the government and the whole country. Not to mention major influence in almost every other country on earth. Masterminds would rule through technology.

Needless to say, it was going to take something very dramatic to reverse the momentum that the C3P had put into motion. It looked like dark days were ahead for the electorate and salad days for the elite.

CHAPTER 6

A Mountain Expedition

During the two years since the C3P administration came to power, the ATP continued to pursue their ability to solidify a new movement within the party. It was obvious, however, that a strangle hold over the citizens was growing because of the technological advances that were consuming the general population. Also though tedious in the ability to wrangle information out of the current administration due to a biased media and censored journalistic releases, the only means of knowing anything was through John's contact, Whisper. Whisper became cooperative as he recognized something was amiss, but he had to walk softly to avoid suspicion toward him as a possible informant to the outside world.

Whisper discovered that yes, what was going on at the mountain was suspicious and suggested that John pursue an operative approach to find out what was really going on. Presenting his conversations with Whisper to *The*

Group, John was authorized to form a team to investigate the mountain for what it was. The only way to accomplish this was to find a group of individuals who could work their way up the mountain and find a means to penetrate what was now to be the C3P headquarters. Not known by anyone yet as the C3P's new headquarters, *The Group* suspected that something very alarming was going on.

John knew several individuals who had retired from the intelligence community and were known as *moles* when they were active in the service. Being *moles*, they had steel nerves and knew how to operate in tight situations. Some specifically had special talents, and though now more mature in age, they still had the physical vigor for such a job. John knew they were sympathetic with the ATP principles and would be anxious to contribute. So selecting three individuals, he called them together to form a plan. Additionally, they would need one individual who was an accomplished mountain climber if they faced unexpected severe terrain.

John called the group *Apex*. Apex was to scale the mountain, find a means of entrance, mix in with the personnel employed in whatever was going on in the facility, and then return to report on their findings. Since the area they were to surveil was watched by security personnel, it was going to be tricky, unless they could pass themselves off as security guards too. One of the first things to do was to find out what security service was looking after the site. This was done by sending someone up to the gated entrance to the site, as though lost, to determine the security service involved. This was easily done; the hard part was gaining entrance by sneaking in from the opposite side of the mountain. It was looking like they would have to rappel into the compound once they got to the entrance side.

The Apex team would spend several days planning their approach and training all to rappel, if necessary, to get into the complex. Getting to the back end of the mountain was not looked at as that difficult, but getting up and around was the major challenge to start with, and the real difficult challenge will be merging into the workforce now entering the mountain and not being detected as interlopers.

On the big kickoff day, the Apex team entered the mountain area and hiked up to the designated target. On the compound entrance site, the terrain was steep, and the weather was beginning to change. A cold misty rain began to fall. This was bad, but it would give them additional cover because security would be hard put to observe all that was going on, and the closed-circuit TV cameras would be misted up. One by one, the Apex team rappelled down one of the steep drops, and fortunately, it was the only one they would encounter.

Dropping onto the compound entrance area, they quickly changed into security guard uniforms and approached the first guard shack. Immediately two security guards approached the group and questioned their presence. The Apex group surrounded the two, jumped them, and injected them with a hypnotic sleeping serum. When they woke, not only would they not remember anything that happened, they would think they had fallen asleep at their station because one would be at his desk, the other would be slouched in a chair. This was designed to make sure there was no suspicion of anyone penetrating the compound without permission.

Knowing already what the check-in process was, the Apex operatives acting as the real security guards began to process personnel as they entered the compound. For some reason, some of the personnel seemed to have lost or misplaced their security badges. During the entrance process, the Apex operatives were able to lift the badges during security searches, and they would later use them to penetrate further into the compound.

Shedding their security uniforms, the Apex group merged with the other personnel in the compound. They split their group into two, two-man teams, each to surveil all they could possibly see and return at a designated time, walking out of the compound as workers, leaving work for the day. Surprisingly, they left the compound without incident. A car had been sent to the compound entrance at the designated time to pick them up, and off they went.

When *The Group* met the next day, the Apex team was able to convey all that they had observed.

Jocko was one of the Apex team, and he spelled out everything they had seen.

"The inside is still under some final construction, so security, though present, hasn't incorporated all of the security checkpoints that will probably be in place when the facility is completed. For that reason, we were able to at least get a general idea of what is taking place. It is obviously not a nuclear waste facility. There is a big building the size of an Amazon warehouse inside the mountain. In the building is a huge area where apparently a large computer and data storage structure is in place. There are large cables to the structure indicating power hookup from the main power source. Adjacent to the computer structure is what I would call a control room with large wall-mounted monitors. Workstations are located in various formations as though representative of an organization of responsibilities according to some method of control and communication. It all looks eerily representative of a megalomaniac's dream of totalitarianism and the means to accomplish it. I would say they should have it completed within a year."

Daniel Solomon, visibly concerned about the mountain enclave, decided that they must increase the activity associated with informing the public on the ATP's implementation of their points on reconciling the party and the vision of the new movement taking place within the ATP to protect the freedom of the people. Once the C3P put into full operation their system of technological control over the nation, no longer will the government be the servant of the people; the people will be slaves of the government, managed through technology. This must not happen.

Daniel said, "Just imagine your family having your children manipulated by computers to believe that the government is responsible for their welfare, not their mom or dad. Imagine every man woman and child so dependent on technological devices to make decisions about everything that they become so dumbed down and that only a manipulative elite decides everything for them through programmed solutions. Imagine the media drumming a partisan line of propaganda through these devices until the individual conscience is destroyed."

So it was time to go public with the Articles of Reconciliation. *The Group* decided now or never. Joanna was instructed to release the articles through her trusted communication sources. Within a week, the news was flashed across the country and the world. Of course, the old-line ATP members were infuriated, by this seemingly unconscionable schism, but once confronted with the reality of the mountain enclave and what appeared to be a conspiracy to convert to a technocratic government, they saw no alternative but to accept reality.

In fact, by accepting the articles, they essentially cleansed themselves from the old ATP, and a new ATP came into being. They wouldn't even have to change their name. They would refresh the public by becoming a new image of transparency and trust. This transparency and trust would be counter to the seemingly mysterious, secretive, and manipulative C3P, now ready to become the T2P that the population would be at a loss to know as to exactly what that meant.

CHAPTER 7

A Techno World

The world over the last ten years had become so dependent on computers, in the hand, on the desk, and on the lap, that to be without one left people feeling incomplete. So ingrained in their heads was their need to have the latest and greatest that they upgraded their devices at every innovation that came into existence. Eventually, a new idol emerged. Technology. Invented by scientists to improve man's lot, corrupted by man to destroy his conscience. Independent thought and God-based faith or hope would no longer be the destiny of man if zealots had their way.

Now technology would replace individual pursuit of happiness, with government-controlled ideals. Sadly, the people, so long dependent in so many ways on government dependency programs, had begun to accept the socialist, liberal, and progressive direction as their destiny. It was a bad omen—a paganistic system that was certain to arouse the wrath of Providence. Just as in the Bible, when

Abraham, Isaac, Jacob, Moses, Aaron, David, and Solomon disappointed God, there was a consequence. When people of Babel, Sodom, and Gomorrah became corrupted, there was a consequence. Any time a covenant was made with God's chosen and the covenant was broken, there was a consequence. After the signs brought on by war in the nineteenth and twentieth century and now a warning brought on by the pandemic in the twenty-first century, was there now to be a greater consequence, perhaps even a chastisement?

The C3P completed their mountain compound by the second year of their party's administration. Controlling all aspects of the party, they now announced that they would change the name of their party to the Technocratic Progressive Party. To be known as the T2P, they would implement every known means of technological control over the operations of government and convey to the people of the country that their security depended on the government's knowledge of everything that was going on in the country and the world. That, in fact, no one goes unnoticed. It was also the intent of the government that every means of communication would be processed through a central exchange that would see to it that law and order was maintained among the electorate and that freedom of speech would be censored so as to convey to the general population that only legitimately sanctioned news would prevail. The failure to follow the government line of communication would be an affront to the state, and they left unclear what the consequence would be.

Needless to say, there was an outcry. But surprisingly, the C3P electorate followers of the time had so aligned themselves with the party that they looked upon this as a sweeping victory for socialism, liberalism, and progressivism. They were lulled into the beliefs of what totalitarianism would give them. They were willing to adore a golden calf rather than a belief in a *one nation under God*.

CHAPTER 8

Reconciliation

As the ATP circulated their *Articles of Reconciliation* throughout the country, it was clear that the minority party was establishing a new awakening for the people. As organizations, town hall meetings, and religious groups began to promote a new wind of freedom, there was still the odor of dismissal, distortion, vile accusations, and threats from the T2P and its media minions against all who wanted to embrace true democratic principles. Since the technocrats controlled the communication outlets, they censored everything the ATP wished to represent and pushed their own propaganda.

A new general election was coming up, and the T2P wanted to dominate the results. They would then have a free hand in completely socializing the country under totalitarian rule.

The ATP, however, found out about the possibility that the president everyone in the country was seeing, primarily through TV and Internet services, was not all that it seemed. It was maybe time for another clandestine operation. This one would take some doing. So *The Group* decided to meet on their island in the sun and hammer out a plan of action.

Daniel started the meeting by having John explain some new revelations he has heard through his contacts in the intelligence community.

John started by saying, "There is the feeling in the government that we really don't have a living president. That we are led on by the creation of a virtual president that is the product of technological wizardry. A phenomenon created, through the digital fabrication of a person, in the image of the president. Everything about him is electronic, none of him is real. There is also the possibility that the real president is dead, and what the people are seeing in the public arena are doubles. Therefore, the power behind the T2P, the tech, mainstream media, social media, and communication moguls are the ones running the government. We are going to be *hard put* to counter what these powerful entities are doing to dominate public thinking."

Daniel intervened by saying, "This all may be true. But it doesn't matter, whether it is or isn't. We are so against what is happening to the country that we must take a more proactive approach to what's ahead of us. We don't have the technological clout the government now has to get the election results we so sorely need. It appears they will win this election, and if they do, we will be simply outlawed as conflicting with the principles the apparent voting population has agreed to accept. We need to increase awareness through the organization we now have in place and hope to God that the interest in the *Articles of Reconciliation* grows as the tyranny of this government shows its ugly face. Then may our time come."

It was the decision of *the Group* that it is time to put the pressure on for all members of the party to promote in every way possible, the *Articles of Reconciliation*, and to issue a warning as to the consequences of lost freedom. This included house-to-house campaigning since media means was practically impossible.

CHAPTER 9

A Cosmic Deliverance

It's not known when or how they came about, but somehow, they were created and traveled through space at a phenomenal speed. Each the size of a small moon many miles in length, width, and depth, these asteroids move through space taking eons to complete their orbits. Traveling from the far side of the sun, astronomers view them seldom as they pass across the face of the sun so infrequently, they are barely noticed. However, these two asteroids have one thing in common, they pass through each other's orbit, which means that in time, they will collide. It's just a matter of when one or the other catches up to the point of intersection. It just so happens that this event is about to take place. And it will happen when they meet between the earth and sun, still deep in space, but with results that will change the earth as we know it today.

Traveling at one hundred fifty thousand to one hundred sixty thousand miles per hour in one thousand hours, they travel over one hundred fifty million miles through space. So when these two asteroids collide, it will be an unbelievable event. Colliding at an impact speed of three hundred thousand miles per hour will create an explosion of such immensity that atoms will split and the huge release of energy will cause an electromagnetic pulse (EMP) of immense proportions. The pulse will travel outward toward everything in space before it. Since the earth will be exposed to this explosion, even though a long distance away, the EMP will travel toward the earth at great speed. Unlike a nuclear bomb exploding in near-earth space which will only affect the earth at a line-of-sight spot on earth, this massive impulse will envelope the whole world like a stone passing through a curtain of water. Everything will be affected even deep into the ground or sea.

*****

Just before the general election occurs in the United States, the two asteroids collide. The EMP passes through space and envelopes the whole earth. Every electronic and electromechanical device is permanently disabled. Every electrical circuit is shorted or destroyed. All data storage, computer chips, and memory devices are wiped clean and rendered totally inoperable, including every spare part or device that could be used to replace or repair any existing item. Everything stops. Everything that uses electrical devices becomes inert.

The immediate result of this occurrence is horrendous. Every car, truck, train, and plane stops in its tracks. Planes fall out of the sky. Ships at sea lose all navigational as well as onboard propulsion or power generation capability. The EMP has even altered magnetic North. Satellites orbiting the earth are no longer functional, including the space station; all on board are doomed. Though the pulse doesn't affect most people long enough to do severe bodily damage, the collateral damage due to explosions of electrically activated armaments and shorts in areas of volatile gases and liquids kills or injures many. Property damage from fire is extreme. People with pacemakers for their heart or people who have underlying medical ailments may succumb to the shock effects brought on by the disaster. A catastrophe just short of Armageddon is about to take place throughout the world.

*****

When the pulse hits, the power grid and all power-generating plants go down. Instrumentation controlling all aspects of electrical power generation is wiped out. Atomic power plants begin to melt down due to lack of cooling capability. Generators are shorted out and are inoperable. Massive power outage takes place all over the planet. Electric lighting becomes a thing of the past. All equipment requiring electricity or that operates electrically will not function for two reasons. No electricity, and all motors will be shorted out and dysfunctional. Pumping equipment will not work, so water and wastewater facilities will be shut down. Without water, toilets will not work; water faucets will not run. Central heating and air-conditioning will come to a halt. Refrigeration and electric utilities will be useless. Elevators in tall buildings will be idle. Subway systems will no longer operate. Telephone switching centers, landlines, and cell phones will be destroyed. Cell towers will be standing relics of the past. There will be no such thing as wireless communication.

*****

Because of the loss of electrical power, much of industry will be idled, if not all. Manufacturing plants will not be able to produce anything except by manual means. Food-processing plants will be limited to manual labor to make available food items. Packaging goods will be rapidly used up, followed by archaic means of wrapping and storing food. The whole food distribution system will have to be restructured. Drug companies will be unable to mass produce their products for the medical industry. Hospitals will be wards only, with no ability to provide oxygen or instrumentation to monitor states of health. Operations will have to take place through antiquated means.

CHAPTER 10

The Aftermath

On that fateful day, Sam Butterworth headed up the mountain to the Palomar Observatory where he spent his shift alone, watching the stars. An astronomer of long standing and passionate about his profession, he studied, charted, and tracked anything that moved in space. Usually starting at an early hour, this morning seemed especially dark and gloomy. At that altitude, it was chilly, and when he pulled into his parking spot, he hustled out of the car to get into the building out of the cold. Setting himself up in his favorite position at the telescope, he began to scan the universe. His usual sites were as expected, but when the sun came up, he scanned between the earth and sun, and he noticed two asteroids moving toward one another.

Not able to recognize their orbit, it looked like they would collide. Knowing, from this distance, that it was not immediately possible to know if they were on a collision course, he would not calculate their relative relationship to each other just now. He gave it little credence. And suddenly, there was a blinding flash. Within moments, Sam felt the building shutter, a burning sensation went through his body, and then everything in the building went dark. His smartphone light should give him at least some light to see with, but it wouldn't turn on.

Groping his way out of his chair and then down the stairs to the main level, he found his way by memory to the exit door. There was the acrid smell of an electrical burn, and smoke had filled the room. Coughing, he left the building and went straight to his car with the idea he would drive back to the city, but his key didn't work to unlock the door. The car wouldn't have started anyway since the starter was shorted, and the electrical control module in the car was burned out by the EMP. With the inability to start the car, he had no alternative but to walk down from the mountain to find somebody to contact.

Sometime later when he finally reached the bottom, he found cars idle in place. People were milling around, wondering what happened. Many thought maybe a nuclear device was detonated by some enemy and it rendered everything inert. It was then that Sam realized that the collision in space must have emitted a massive electromagnetic pulse. To allay fears of an atomic incursion by a hostile foreign country, he immediately passed his belief among the crowd. It wasn't long, and everybody realized that this was a phenomenon that was going to affect every aspect of their life. The world was just set back two hundred fifty years, about the same time as when the USA declared its independence. Isn't it ironic? It was almost as though the country was going to get a second chance at doing it right, as its founder's intended.

*****

Washington, DC, the center of federal government in the United States, was shaken to its core, not by an earthquake but by the enormity of electronic destruction of its vital means of carrying out government business. Congress was stripped of its ways to communicate, and politicians were unable to carry out their responsibilities, since the halls and offices of administrative and collaborative activity were all but blackened out. Much had to be done to bring about an organized means of carrying out government activity.

In the meantime, there was also the problem of the fact that there was really no living president, and the actual vice president and speaker of the house were killed in an earthquake disaster occurring on the west coast. The virtual president was the one who was on the ballot for the general election. In reality, there was no incumbent president on the ballot, except in name only. The new T2P, without anyone in control, had to either reveal that there was no real president or take advantage of the communication blackout and proceed as though there was a real president. In any case, the party was in total disarray. Somehow, Congress had to be called together to determine how to carry out government business until the election of the next administration.

*****

When the EMP hit New York City, everything shut down. It occurred right at morning rush hour, and the roads were clogged with every kind of vehicle dead in its place. Not only were people getting out of their useless vehicles, all of the high-rise buildings began disgorging their occupants onto the streets. It was absolute chaos. With everything shut down, people were at a loss as to what was happening. Being one of the largest cities on earth, the magnitude of disaster was overwhelming. With the conveniences of the modern world shut down, big cities all over the world were impacted the greatest.

Without power, utilities, water, sewer, or communication, everything became an unruly mess. Where do you go to get drinking water? Where do you go to relieve yourself? Where do you go to get help of any kind? Garbage would build up in the streets. These were the threats the population was facing everywhere. But none were so affected as much as the major cities. The government was useless because they had no means of doing much of anything under the circumstances. Police and fire departments were without vehicles and equipment to either manage looting or putting out fires. Bicycles and horses were the only means of getting around, and they served to provide some ability to exercise a modicum of control, arbitrary at best.

But one of the bigger impacts the EMP had was the shutting down of the banking and financial entities, not only in New York City but around the world, so dependent on computers and communication. Unless hard copy records were accessible, all data were erased, not to mention the software programs used to process information. Not only was the stock market nonfunctional, all computer records of accounts were deleted and not recoverable. Credit cards, debit cards, and all plastic financial mediums were useless. ATMs no longer functioned. Without factual information, people conceivably could lose everything, and the wealthiest would be hit the hardest. The panic that ensued was many times worse than at any time in history.

Unlike small cities and towns where people came together to overcome any disaster, the large cities had such huge diverse populations that it couldn't get itself organized to meet the chaos as readily as small towns. Since gangs and less-than-honest citizens were more numerous, they pillaged and looted to serve themselves rather than being contributors to the needs of the citizenry. Citizens with guns could protect themselves; those without could not. Without law enforcement, the thieves and thugs exploited the disaster for their own ends adding to the suffering of others. A form of anarchy prevailed. The big cities began to disintegrate as people left the large cities in droves, seeking out more compassionate and cooperative environments.

*****

Small towns and rural areas made out a lot better than the bigger cities. Though everything was thrown in disarray, people recognizing the disaster for what it was began to come together to help each other out. Meeting in the churches and community centers, they planned out the means to cope with the dilemma. Rather than relying on the government, which could do nothing, groups began forming restoration projects to dig wells and construct outhouses or septic tanks for the population so they would have some means of maintaining hygiene. Communication was in the form of letters and messengers. Food items were distributed at open air vegetable stands, while butchering of animals for food were supplied at local butcher shops. Farmers brought their goods into the towns to distribute. Since mediums of exchange were in question or scarce, trade and bartering was a dominant means used for acquiring goods and services.

*****

Travel would now revert to the eighteenth century, with horses, horse and buggy, and bicycles as means of transportation. In other parts of the world, donkeys, mules, camels and other beasts of burden would be used for travel or to provide heavy-duty muscle power to do burdensome work. Fortunately, steam power being mechanical, the old *iron horse* could be put into service to haul on the countries' railroad network, coal, passengers, iron ore, petroleum, and food items. Antiquated steam engines would be used as tractors, on steam shovels, pumping from wells, steamboats, and the basis for recreating the means to restore many services, but it would take time, since everything had to be built or restored from scratch. Sails for boats and sailing vessels would come back into use in a big way. People coming together with hope and dedication, reliant on the grace of God, would start putting things back together. And it would take a lot of faith. Once again, the churches were filled with people who realized that what took place was no ordinary event.

*****

Because of the EMP, all military throughout the world were affected. Planes couldn't fly, tanks couldn't run, rocket engines could not be ignited, artillery pieces would work if they were stand-alone, but there were no mobile guns, and horses or manpower would have to pull the guns. As long as there was ammunition, rifles and pistols would still work. However, the means to haul troops and supplies was hampered by the lack of mobile equipment. Ships at sea and submarines had lost all of their navigational devices, except manual instruments to guide by the stars and sun, but true North had to be found again in order to determine direction. These navigational items wouldn't be of much use anyway, since none of the ships or subs could operate. Many just floundered at sea or sank. ICBMs lost all of their targeting instrumentation, and the engines could not be fired. In truth, the world's military powers became neutralized to the point that no one nation could exercise power over another.

*****

Manufacturing throughout the world came to a standstill, except handmade goods. Any, and all, production requiring electrical mediums was nullified since nothing worked. The big tech companies were defunct overnight. Internet-mailing houses were totally put out of business. Media enterprises were silenced. Mills that used waterpower to turn waterwheels could still operate through their system of gears and pulleys, but high-production facilities using electric means to operate computerized or electrified production equipment or robots were rendered useless. Electrical power would have to be assembled from scratch, and the means to get all that was required to do just that would have to be gathered and made by hand. Steam power would be the stepping stone to powering equipment.

*****

Mass media communication all but ceased. Printed media could only be done by mechanically typesetting and hand-cranked printing presses would have to be found somewhere to be able to print pages. Paper was in short supply because the paper mills ceased to run.

All radio and TV communications were stilled. The entertainment industry came to a halt, and movie actors and actresses along with the industry itself were at a standstill. Once wealthy movie idols or producers, now they were just everyday people without jobs.

Cross-country communication would eventually be by telegraph, if enough good wire could be found to extend connections to distant locations. Batteries could be made with glass jars of acid and lead for those clever enough to make rudimentary means of producing electricity. Morse code was to be the method of communication, and telegraphers would be highly sought to operate telegraph machines.

*****

When the EMP hit, *The Group* were on their Caribbean Island. Realizing something drastic had happened, because all island-powered equipment had ceased operating and their phone and computers were no longer operable, they decided they would leave the island. But when they tried to start their boat's motor, nothing happened. Fortunately, they had a sailing vessel and considered using it to get to the mainland. They soon discovered that they had no sea guidance that worked, and the compass seemed off phase, pointing North in a direction that was obviously wrong. It was obvious to them that seemingly some intergalactic force had neutralized everything.

Realizing they needed to assess the situation they were in, they decided to check their island resources to see how they could survive and for how long. Fortunately, they had fuel reserves stored on the island so they could keep lanterns going for lighting. There were some matches, but they decided to keep a perpetual flame lit to have a way to keep candles and lanterns as well as any heating or cooking that needed to be done. They had rooftop cisterns that were full of water, and rains would keep them filled. They had running water from the cisterns to operate their toilets, and the water from the cistern could be boiled to make the water pure. Septic tanks had long been used on the island.

After assessing their situation, they found that with food from the sea and bananas and cocoanuts plus planted fruit and vegetables on the island, they could stay for quite a length of time. They did, however, plan to go to the mainland at some point as soon as they could figure out how to chart a course across the open sea without navigation equipment and especially a reliable compass. It would finally come down to the stars and sun showing them the way.

*****

For *The Committee*, they were all in their mountain compound when the EMP hit. Their massive technological enclave to control the country and even parts of the world had been completed, and they were working to direct everything to an intended totalitarian rule. When the pulse hit, their power sources and supercomputers developed massive short circuits and burst into flame. A great deal of plastic associated with the computers as well as wiring caused dense acrid smoke. Because they were housed in the mountain, fire consumed the oxygen, and the smoke was so dense, it actually caused death by smoke inhalation and suffocation.

The heat was massive, and since water-sprinkling systems were fed by water pumps, the pumps were shorted out and couldn't operate. No means of stifling the fire was possible, and everybody within the enclave was killed or consumed by fire. Like the C3P before them, all were annihilated, and the power behind the new T2P ceased to exist. Finally, a force greater than man himself had destroyed an aspiring power of evil. It would seem that the country and possibly the world was now free of forces that relied on money, power, and technology to implement self-serving man-made ideologies.

*****

One of the outstanding results of the EMP was the devastation it caused on the west coast of America and along the *Ring of Fire* throughout the world. In California, aside from the fires caused by the blowing up of transformers and the resultant forest fires that consumed millions of acres, another phenomenon occurred. For some reason, the EMP affected the tectonic plate movement on the planet. Volcanic action increased, and earthquakes in critical areas caused the earth to split open wherever faults existed. One of the hardest hit places was along the San Andreas Fault on the Western part of the United States. San Francisco and surrounding cities were hit so hard that people were rapidly evacuated by any means possible. The area was turned into a mass of rubble, and fires burned everywhere. The fault line opened, the sea rushed in, flooding so far inland that it was as though part of California had fallen into the Pacific Ocean. The Golden Gate Bridge collapsed on its southern end.

This destruction occurred all the way to Los Angeles where earthquakes of such magnitude caused the city to see its high-rise buildings collapse, and conflagrations consumed much of the city.

Yellowstone National Park, nothing more than an ancient caldera, began to erupt in a way that changed the landscape of the entire park. Geysers that were once landmarks of regular displays ceased to exist, and earthquakes presaged what might be the beginnings of destructive explosions of major consequence. Wildlife, so prevalent before, seemed to disappear from the area as though something terrible was expected.

Worldwide there was an increase in volcanic action, and this increased the amount of ash in the air by such an extent that the world actually cooled from the reduced radiation from the sun. It was expected that winters would be colder than normal, and it was not out of the realm of possibility that an *ice age* could occur.

The damage caused by earthquakes, volcanoes, and tsunamis throughout the world and the collateral destruction associated with these events, in some way, were going to touch the lives of every person on earth.

CHAPTER 11

The Tale of Two Cities

If you lived in a big city, life is far different than if you lived in a small city. If you live in New York City, it means you dwell among swarms of residents all rushing to get where they're going either walking, by subway, taxi, or bus. Children can usually walk to school if it's in walking distance. Working parents either walk or ride the train or bus. Life is a constant state of coming or going at a rapid pace. There is little time to converse, so on the busy street or on a subway train, people are relatively cold to one another.

Familiarity seems to be avoided since there always seems to be the suspicion of ulterior motives. And there is the familiar *in-your-face* way that New Yorkers converse. Additionally, New Yorkers as a majority like the liberality that is present in a large city where every form of dining, entertainment, visual sights, and sounds as well as vice and corruption abound, everyone seems to be on the *take* since *pay-to-play* schemes from getting into a restaurant, politics, law enforcement, job security, or doing business is the order of the day.

Instead of a mingling between ethnic groups, ghettos are formed either to protect themselves or to form a bloc to influence self-serving interests. Sometimes even these ghettos feed upon themselves instead of serving the very people who they should be looking after. Sometimes they become so lawless that they kill their own for some selfish anarchistic desire, or they foster gangs to carry out paganistic club objectives. And, with a large percentage of the city population on the dole compared to smaller cities, it is this very state of existence that is ripe for totalitarianism.

It may be different in other big cities, but they all seem to have a similar mix of inhabitants, forming ghettos or monoethnic sections of town serving their own set of values rather than being part of a more cooperative and united community. Racism isn't a one-way street. All ethnic groups have within their sphere those who are just as racist to their opposites and in the same radical ways. Some even exploit the idea that they are alone in being biased against either by propaganda, ignorance, or as a means to an immoral end.

*****

Rural areas and small- to medium-size towns have a slower and more casual lifestyle. They're friendlier, and by and large are more outgoing and warmer to others. Because they are more involved with each other on an everyday basis in their community, it's easier for them to come together in times of need. If you conducted a poll comparing big city people to rural or smaller town or village people, you would find that by a great margin, big city people would be considered colder, more aloof, and less considerate of others. In times of an emergency, smaller town people band together to overcome adversity.

In the big cities, the people depend on first responders, and if they don't respond, it's the first responder's fault, not that of the people in general. Therein lies the problem. Big city people look to others to solve their problems and think that government should be the solution. Smaller cities look to each other to get through difficult times. That's why, when a calamity such as this intergalactic force that shuts down everything comes about, the rural and smaller cities will survive much better and be able to provide goods and services almost immediately in some way or kind. Many times, because of a greater belief in God, they have faith and hope and carry out responsibility through charity as a sign of love for all mankind not just a love of self.

CHAPTER 12

A New Beginning

Imagine yourself being caught up in a world purged of every electrical device invented by man. Mankind is thrust back two hundred fifty years when physical labor and the use of animals were the mode of everyday living. However, there has been a massive cleansing of the world. Nuclear devices no longer work; corrupt financial, technical, and media industries are neutralized. Government used as a power monger to harass the citizenry and tax, tax and double tax to satisfy the ever-increasing demands of government overspending is at an end. The rich have lost control of their wealth and therefore their influence both in political purposes and in the private sector. The playing field is leveled; everybody is in the same boat. But who copes best? That isn't hard to figure.

Those who lived a modest life and earned a living honestly and conscientiously cope very well. Those who were indolent and relied on government handouts are now destitute. The poor who had little, know what being without is like, can assimilate into the present circumstances with everybody else. The rich are the ones who are unable to cope. So used to the luxuries of life, many become so despondent that they commit suicide at the realization of their loss. Truly, the last have become first and the first last. And there is a new exodus, as people move from the big cities to the small cities or rural life. Like giant ice cubes, the big cities are melting away. Who wants to live in the filth and chaos of so many people where solutions aren't solved by compassion and care for one another? Who wants to live where you are threatened every day by muggers and thieves who live their life by looting and killing or by a local government run by fraud, corruption, and pay to play?

There is unfortunate fallout to innocent people. Those who worked their whole life and now retire on social security or pension funds no longer receive their monthly payments. The same is true of those on disability. But there is always hope that family and friends will look out for many of them, especially if they belonged to churches or social community groups who certainly would reach out to help them.

On the bright side, there is a whole new opportunity. Relying on the original constitution of the United States, the country can try again to establish its *one nation under God* full of hope and opportunity. Unfettered by radical ideologies and armed with hope and moral vision, the country can build itself up to an even better place. Its ideology was formed in 1776, and all that needs to be done is to carry it through to its original intent. *The Group* had planted the seeds throughout the country with their *Articles of Reconciliation* before the calamity that was distributed through a network of cities, towns, and villages. Many people chose these tenets as the means to a new beginning—establishing an authority that served the people, not themselves.

CHAPTER 13

A Clean Sweep

The entire earth was fundamentally changed as a result of the forces of Providence. It would now have to remake itself since the playing field was essentially leveled for everybody. Little by little, each nation found some means of putting things back together. Ironically, the poorer nations had suffered more by natural occurrences than the effects of the loss of electronic and electrical devices. Used to living by primitive means, they adapted quickly. Whereas the once affluent nations found themselves struggling on how to cope with archaic means of survival.

Nothing was truer than in the bigger cities of the United States. Left with no electrical means of power and everything requiring manual labor, the large cities faced greater deprivation. With garbage and waste growing in the streets of the city, a stench pervaded everything. This coupled with looting and the means to provide safe shelter, especially during the winter, made survival almost unbearable. Finding enough horsepower to haul supplies to the central city to feed and provide life support essentials was a big problem.

So the residents did the only thing they could do, they began to leave. So many left that the city found itself without reliable citizens to reestablish their community. The looters, thieves, and hoodlums took over, block by block, sections of the city establishing their own method of control over the citizens, a form of cruel martial law. It wasn't long, and evil leaders began to carve out areas of the city they wished to control, and soon there was war between these devious enclaves. Soon the whole city devolved into an abandoned wasteland of burned-out buildings, scarred edifices, and decayed symbols of the past. What was needed was a citizenry to manage the creation of a new city from the rubble of a bygone age. Who or what was going to bring that about was yet unknown.

Things were different in the outlying parts of the country. Small towns came together to form some semblance of law and order and organized themselves to help one another. Ingenuity coupled with manual labor brought about the means to provide food and supplies to the city. Farmers, still able to plant crops, raise animals, and reap and distribute food items, soon adapted to the new reality. Special effort was made to increase the breeding of animals for food or for animal power to pull plows or provide travel means. Since relics of steam-powered engines and tractors still found in farms and museums, engineers and mechanics began to put these relics back into action, and iron smiths provided the means to make anything required for steel fabrication. Some old water mills still had old machinery that functioned as lathes or drilling machines. Putting them into use allowed the creation of many items to replace that which no longer worked.

When the crisis hit, all financial means of transaction was practically annihilated. The usual means of exchange in the form of money was stifled. What do you use that has value when banks, financial institutions, and the like are shut down? Gold, silver, precious metals, and gems can be used, but since the average person is not able to determine worth under the circumstances, what is a unit of measure? Even they have dubious value until a standard is set, and who will do that? Well, maybe paper money can still be used since the average everyday person knows how to count? As a medium of exchange, regardless of what it is backed by, as long as it can be used in trade, it has value.

Sooner or later, if a central government comes about, it's easier to trade paper money than to trade precious metals. At least in the near term, paper money is used for those who have it. Those who have had financial wealth in the form of stock as a virtual accumulation saved in a data bank have nothing to trade. Therefore, they become the poor because of the lack of cash. If the once wealthy still have their precious metals and gems, they will see the limitation as a means of exchange until they get someone to convert it to cash if cash is accepted as a more viable means of exchange. Once gold, silver, and gems are used up, all the equipment to mine these items has stopped. Only pick, shovel, and panning will bring some means of mining for metals of value. It will take some time before all this is worked out.

All across the continent, the people in the smaller towns and rural areas came together to solve their problems. The big cities suffered. No longer did political faction play a part in everyday living, since everybody was in the same boat. But since the American Traditional Party's *Articles of Reconciliation* had been distributed throughout the United States, it's tenets made more sense to the general population. Now it was a matter of putting those tenets into action since it more readily identified with the intentions of the original founders of our nation and what brought such great opportunity to our ancestors in the making of America.

What happened when this cataclysm came about was a wake-up call that deviating from *In God We Trust* was an ideology that was against every truth created for man that was good and holy? Now was the opportunity for a second chance. And this chance meant that there must be not one party but more than one party, using the principles established by the founders, to see to it that no one party has greater influence over the other but that they must coexist as organs of the citizenry. That, at all times, they must act as servants for the good of the people based on God-based moral grounds. To do otherwise would be an act of self-serving interest and would defy the principles established by the Constitution and therefore not qualified to represent its citizenry.

CHAPTER 14

A Matter of Convenience

Before the EMP changed everything, people were so used to the modern conveniences that it never occurred to them what it would be like if they were all taken away. Just look into your life and see what life would be like once your modern conveniences were taken away. Take for example, the Adams family and their three children.

While the rush hour was picking up steam on the east coast, in the Midwest where it was still dark, when the EMP hit, suddenly all power went out. Not realizing what happened, Mr. Adams checked the breakers. The flashlight didn't work, so he used a match to see the circuit breakers. They were blown, but when reset, they didn't work anyway. So they searched for some candles to give the house some light. Figuring there was a power outage, the father and his wife got the kids up to go to school. Then they found out the water wasn't running, and when the kids went to the bathroom, the toilets wouldn't flush.

At this point, they decided to turn on the TV news to see what was going on but realized that wasn't going to work. So they decided to use the cell phone, but that didn't work either. They had a computer, but it also did not function, even on batteries. At the same time, they also realized that their central heating/air-conditioning system was not going to work either, and the house was becoming uncomfortable. Going out to the car, they found out it wouldn't start. Looking around outside, it was obvious all the neighbors were in the same fix. After talking with each other in the neighborhood, they realized it was no use to send the kids to school and why go to work if there's no way to get there. There also was an eerie silence in the air because nothing was moving. What was missing was the usual hum of equipment, cars, and trucks and the occasional train whistle and ambulance sirens.

Though the Adams family had some food in the house, the refrigerator was not working, and they couldn't prevent anything from spoiling. Also the dishes in the dishwasher that wasn't run last night would not work this morning. A load of clothes that were to be washed in the next day or two were not going to get washed except by some means other than by clothes washer. Plus where was all the water going to come from to wash and clean. The gravity of the situation began to sink in.

So Mr. Adams took one of the children's bicycles and road to the nearest police station to see what was going on. Of course, the police station was just as inoperable as everything else. Soon word of mouth got around that something had happened in space, and it affected everything on earth.

Mr. Adams went home and realizing that somehow, some way, he had to take care of his family. While returning from the police station he passed the bank. People were lined up at the ATM machine to get cash, but it wasn't working, and the bank itself was not open since all the computers were down.

Grocery stores were open, but they were running out of everything, and cash was the only acceptable medium of exchange since credit cards, debit cards, and checks were not accepted. The store could sell dry goods, but they were rapidly running out of fresh meats and frozen items because their equipment wasn't functioning either, and it was only a matter of time when they would have to throw things away. So as the stores approached the critical time on refrigerated items, they started giving them away rather than dump them.

When Mr. Adams got home, he related to his wife all that he had seen and heard. Together, they decided how to establish a routine for their family until some semblance of community action determined where this situation was going. Meals would be cooked on the barbecue grill until the propane was gone. Cold meals would be used as best as possible, and not knowing how long food would last, meals would be kept at modest levels, no extravagance. Shopping would be on and as needed basis, since finding food items was going to be a problem and means of preserving food was limited. Besides, it was not known how much money was going to be available or if money would even be used as a means of exchange.

Fortunately, the Adams' had a fireplace, so they could burn trash, and if necessary, do some cooking over a fire. Wood was scarce, so they decided they would burn old furniture and use what fuel they had in the yard from tree branches and bushes. Once they were out of fuel, they didn't know exactly what they would do except to pray and hope things would come together to bring about sources of supply. For water, they decided to collect rainwater in tubs and pails. They dug a hole in the backyard for disposal of waste and used a bucket set in the toilet, and chamber pots were made available so they only had to worry about what they would do when they ran out of toilet paper. That was one of the first things grocery stores ran out of, and with paper mills shut down, no expectation of toilet paper supplies was known.

Since the night was now lit by candles or lanterns (for as long as they lasted), the daily routine became rising at first light and going to bed as soon as it was dark. All attention was now centered on survival. Faith-centered families prayed for deliverance and trusted God would show them the way. Non-faith-centered families just wondered where this was all going and spent their time worrying and wondering when the government was going to come to save them. Little did they know that at this point, there was no government. Their reliance on government rather than a God who saves proved their undoing, and those who believed came together and saved each other.

In the major cities, the stress of losing conveniences was a serious problem. If you lived in a high-rise building, the only way to your apartment or condo was by stairs or elevator. Since the elevators didn't work, you had no quick means to get to or out of your unit. Unless you had a deck, you couldn't cook on a barbecue grill. Since you were without water in your unit, you had to bring it in, by bottle or container, and if you lived several stories up, it was difficult. The means to get rid of waste was an ordeal that most people just had a hard time adapting to, since the means of disposal was very limited. Maintaining health and hygiene became a real struggle.

When you did get out on the street, more people were on the street than in their homes. Restaurants ran out of everything in no time, and shops did the same with no expectation of resupply. The streets were littered with trash and inoperable vehicles. Any abandoned car soon was stripped of anything useable, even the fuel tanks were siphoned, including the crankcase of oil. Tires were removed to be used as fuel for fireplaces and in barrels at homeless gatherings. An obnoxious smell of burning rubber mixed with the other smells of garbage, waste, or spoilage pervaded the city. Suicide levels in the major cities outstripped smaller towns by an unimaginable number as big city people couldn't cope, and drug users unable to get drugs went into withdrawal. Those who once were rich couldn't accept their fate and ended their misery by jumping out of windows or off tall buildings.

The rural areas of the country, though used to the same conveniences as *in town* people, they adapted better to the loss of these benefits because they lived closer to the earth. That is, they had the ability to grow food, raise and use animals, and put into use some of their antiquated equipment to harvest crops. They still could use old windmills to pump water from their wells, and the spirit of cooperation between neighbors allowed them to work together to overcome adversity. Masters of fixing things, they improvised to work out problems, and they generally had a greater sense of God's presence in all that they did. They at least could provide for themselves and gradually would provide for others in an ever-increasing way, either as a love of neighbor or as a means of income.

CHAPTER 15

A Return to the Mainland

The Group situated on their island in the sun came to the realization that they must get back to mainland USA. Knowing there would be devastation, they concluded that they might be able to help form a more perfect union by refocusing on the Constitution and the Declaration of Independence and purge the nation of the socialist and totalitarian ideologies that were pervading the nation before the catastrophe.

Perhaps, they could establish a new *Continental Congress* to implement the *Articles of Reconciliation* and limit the power that party politics had come to influence over the citizenry for their own party ends. Equal justice under the law would be their goal for citizen and government office holders as well. No nation can govern itself equitably if there is favoritism to those who govern versus the governed. Government must serve the people, not dominate. The sovereignty of the states should prevail, and the federal government must defend and protect according to the will of the electorate.

But, to even imagine a new beginning, the group had to get to the mainland. Fortunately, they had a sailing vessel on the island. One of this group was a sailing enthusiast and knew how to use a sextant. They always had one onboard ship as a backup, in the event they ever lost power to operate the boat's GPS. Guidance by the stars would get them to their destination.

The Group packed up their belongings and stowed food and water on board the yacht to last the time they thought it would take to get to the mainland, and since they had some fuel for lanterns and an onboard cookstove, they were ready for the trip. They closed down the island and set off for America. It was an adventure they would not soon forget.

Before they left the island, they were able to determine the variance that resulted from the EMP in indicating true North on the compass. So they recalibrated their compass to adjust for the difference. Now, by the use of their maps, compass, and sextant, they were reasonably sure they could sail to their intended destination. Even if they were slightly off on their mainland landing, they could get to where they wanted to go.

So here they were, an ex-President of the United States, his former press secretary, and national intelligence director, plus other associates known among themselves as *The Group*, along with their spouses, all heading for America one thousand five hundred miles away. Fortunately, there were no storms, and the trip was uneventful. Supplementing their onboard food supply with fish caught at sea, water from frequent rains, and sufficient fuel for cooking and light, everybody was kept in a good state of health. Generally moving along at seven to eight knots, they were in sight of mainland USA after a week. They decided to land at or near Charleston, South Carolina, and would decide from there where to settle. Since everything was an unknown, each day would have to be planned according to conditions.

When *The Group* arrived off the coast of South Carolina, they decided they would move up the coast from Charleston, find an inlet, and anchor the boat. Then, using their dinghy, a landing party would set for shore to get a feel as to what was going on. Once they felt secure in going ashore, they would find a means of travel to a preferred destination. Perhaps, they could settle in some abandoned house or if possible, contact a known individual to help them on their way. Echo, Mike, and Whiskey had accumulated, through their network setup, hard copies of the organization they created throughout the country for establishing a following to the *Articles of Reconciliation*. These contacts would be the means of organizing the necessities of a devastated nation. By these means, *The Group* would set about putting together some semblance of authority and discipline from what was complete disorder.

Not too far from Charleston, *The Group* found a nice inlet to drop anchor. It was decided that Daniel Solomon, John Brooks, and Echo would go ashore first to scope out the situation. The rest would remain on board. They had made sure they had pistols and rifles with them when they left the island because they knew they might have to protect themselves or they may have to use them to hunt for food. The shore party took arms and ammunition, plus a backpack, including food, tent, and a map. Those remaining on board were charged with protecting themselves as well as the boat until the party returned. Decisions would then be made as to what the next adventure would be.

Mike rowed the party to shore with the dinghy, bid them good luck, and returned to the boat. It was a cool, damp morning and looked like it might rain. Echo, Daniel, and John tromped inland hoping to find a road. Everything was eerily silent except for the wind, some bird calls, and an occasional sound of a tree branch breaking. Aside from that, no sound of vehicles or the whirr of machinery. They continued to walk, and after about two miles inland, they came to a road. Picking a northerly direction, they headed up the road.

Soon they came upon a car stopped in a ditch. The tires were gone, and the inside of the car was empty of anything loose. The hood was up, and it was obvious the car was ransacked. A little farther along was another car, all stripped. Eventually, after passing many nonfunctioning vehicle remains and trudging along at a steady pace, they came to the outskirts of the city. As they ambled into the town, it was evident that everything was at a standstill. The only things moving were people, and they were searching for places to get food or fuel of some sort to support their daily needs. It appeared they were being cooperative to each other in coping the best they could, since everyone was in the same fix. Echo knew that there was one of the eastern network organizers he had set up, living in this area of town, so they decided to track him down and see what the overall circumstances were. By nightfall, they found his residence and sought to get him to put them up for a while.

This network organizer was Teddy Jones. He had been a political organizer for the ATP for many years and was a serious supporter of the *Articles of Reconciliation* and all that they stood for. Inviting them into his house, he saw to their immediate needs for something to eat and drink, and they all sat down to discuss the situation.

"Things are very bad," claimed Teddy. "We have all we can do to find food, good water, and the needs to meet our daily survival. Nothing works except mechanical devices. It's as if we are living in pioneer days, and everybody is in the same fix. There's a lot of confusion and chaos, and it's going to be necessary to form some kind of organization and authority, to lead people to caring for each other, and to start some semblance of rebuilding. Already, gangs of toughs are trying to rule segments of the city. I've already formed a group of citizens to start the process, and we are meeting again this week. With your presence, I'm sure we will get a lot of cooperation to further our efforts."

With that said, *The Group* from the boat, along with Teddy and his group of followers, set about to form a local means of organizing the city. Staying with Teddy, as long as it was necessary to formulate organizational plans for Teddy to carry out, Daniel and his boat partners headed back to the boat to get the others on shore and to plan their next move. They intended to move up the coast and establish further relationships from Echo's list of followers. By traveling up the coast inland, they wanted to see all that was going on as the people struggled to survive in this new setting that set the country back hundreds of years. At some point, they intended to have representatives from each state meet at an eastern center and begin the fundamentals of putting the country back together again as intended by the original founders.

Returning to their boat in the inlet, Daniel and his cohorts prepared themselves and their families to travel. To start with, walking was a necessity. However, Teddy had given them some names of farmers further to the North who had horses and buggies whereby they may be able to work out arrangements to use them as their means of transportation. It was getting into fall, and the weather was beginning to turn. So they moved out promptly, seeking out from Teddy's list of farmers the families that might help them.

After a long difficult trek, *The Group* managed to reach the first farmer on Teddy's list. The weather had been cold and rainy. Lots of mud, and when they had been traveling, village after village was devastated by the difficult conditions. People were surviving, but faith in the future looked confusing. Daniel and his family and friends would encourage them to take heart. He assured them they would be working to get things back together, but for now, it would be up to them to work out cooperative ways of survival by working compassionately with each other. Faith in God and love of neighbor would get them through.

The first farmer they reached was Basil Baker. He had a farm of one hundred acres and provided most of his own meat, fruits, and vegetables. He had milk cows, beef cows, and several horses. Two for riding, two for pulling a cart or buggy, and four for farmwork. His farm had been in the family for generations, so he had some old mechanical equipment to help him harvest crops.

Basil was a tough crusty old coot, but he had a heart of gold and always looked after his neighbors. He liked Teddy because of what he stood for and dedicated himself to helping Teddy distribute the *Articles of Reconciliation* and anticipated the day they could put all in motion. Seeing this group come to his farm was a welcome opportunity. Recognizing the former president, he wished to cooperate any way he could. He not only put up the entourage that came upon him but provided them with everything they needed to continue their journey North. After a stay of a week, they left with the two riding horses, two horses with one buggy and a wagon, grain for the horses, plenty of food, preserves and water, warm clothes, some utensils for cooking, matches for fires, and candles for lighting. The rest of their needs, they would have to get along the way.

The first day out, the day turned bitter cold. It snowed at first, and when the cold really set in, it was almost sunset. So the party found a spot near a stand of woods where they settled for the evening. The first thing they did was round up firewood to last till morning. Forming a lean-to, they all gathered underneath with a brisk fire burning in front of them, taking advantage of the radiant heat from the fire. The men in the group took turns on watch and kept the fire stoked. They all slept comfortably that first night, despite the cold.

In the morning, a breakfast of eggs, bacon, fresh bread provided by Basil Baker's wife from the day before, and coffee raised spirits and gave all energy to take on the day. It didn't hurt that upon rising in the morning, one of the men saw a deer which he shot. It was a real challenge, since no one knew how to dress a deer. But after figuring out how to hang it from a tree, they managed to gut and skin it. Cutting it up in portions as best they could, the cold weather would keep it fresh and would feed the group for several days or more. Since deer were easily available, meat would be a regular item on this journey.

After a rigorous trek on back roads through ice and snow, the party finally came to an interstate highway. What a sight. Four lanes of highway intermittently cluttered with idle trucks and cars. Semis were dead in their lane, and the doors of the trailer were open. The interiors were empty as they were either looted, or the driver had given away the contents. As the group moved along the interstate, they observed or met other parties traveling the best they could to either get away from where they had been or going to an unknown place of opportunity; not really sure what that might be. Survival was their motivation, and most seemed to help one another.

The Group had by now passed through several towns where Echo had a network representative. Emphasizing the need to incorporate some kind of organizational structure within each community, they moved on to continue that mission and planned to reach Fredericksburg, Virginia, where they hoped to set up a center for establishing a government under the precepts of the *Articles of Reconciliation.*

Only fifty-five miles from Washington, DC, it seemed appropriate to avoid the old center of government, at least for the time being. They would set about solidifying their organizational structure, communicate by whatever means possible to their organization network throughout the rest of the country, and then call for representatives from each state to travel to a designated point where they would bring about a new *Continental Congress* dedicated to bringing back the country to some kind of normality. The EMP had devastated the workings of the federacy so that there was a complete governmental void. A president who wasn't a president, no leadership, a congress that couldn't function, and the states were in a similar disarray. *The Group's* intention was to motivate the country by using the *Articles of Reconciliation* and the Constitution as already established to rally the people into forming *a more perfect union*.

CHAPTER 16

A World in Chaos, A Country in Renewal

Over a period of several months, in America, a formative structure began to evolve in each state as the means of working out ways to rebuild communities became evident. The winters were especially hard, since the worldwide spread of volcanic ash had limited the effects of the sun. Temperatures dropped to never seen record lows, and snowfalls were massive. The global warming scare of the past had completely evaporated. Since all-moving vehicles and industrial emissions were practically eradicated, there was no reason to promote global warming scenarios. What was needed was the ways and means to keep warm. Millions of people throughout the world died from the effects of the bitter cold winters. Summers became a blessing even though the average temperatures were considerably lower than any historical normal. A mini *ice age* was in the making.

Thanks to the renovation of steam locomotives, and the ability to use existing rail lines, coal, and wood products was now being shipped to various parts of the country to help the population heat their homes. Businesses with steam-powered equipment would have resources to run their equipment as they adapted to the production of items necessary to support life. Rail passenger cars provided travel opportunity, and mail communication gradually developed over time. Basic remnants of essentials gradually made their way to the general public, despite the archaic ways and means in which they were brought back to the needy population. It was through faith, hope, and charity by individuals to help each other that made it all happen.

Government, for and by the people, began to establish the rhythm of life into which men came together to solve problems and to rebuild a nation. When you consider that every conceivable electronic device was eradicated, all the labor-saving inventions were no longer available. Toil was the order of the day. What were once simple tasks of operating equipment that did hard physical labor was reverted to back-breaking hardship or meticulous hand labor. What were once electronic devices to communicate, diagnose disease, mass produce essentials, or provide entertainment were now gone.

Individuals with hearing loss could no longer rely on aids to understand conversations. Heart pacemakers ceased to function ending the lives of many. Doctors and dentists could not do X-rays. Tooth decay was resolved by pulling teeth. Emergency operations could only be performed in rudimentary ways with many patients dying. Days were filled with acts of survival and by making sure there was a perpetual flame to cook, heat, and light. What the world had developed in blessings to mankind, mankind failed to acknowledge what power it was that really did provide all of creation and those things that were inspired by God and made through man. By one instant event, all were swept away. Now, by this chastisement, they would either come to a full realization, or there could be another, even more devastating consequence.

There was a great benefit from this current chastisement: the elimination of electronic scams, fraud, cyber-attacks, hacking, robbery of bank accounts by electronic means and fraud, and sales harassment by phone. Out of every bad comes a greater good. But to get this good, a greater price had to be paid.

Around the world, the effects of the EMP hit the totalitarian nations the hardest. These governments, particularly China, succumbed to the total shut down of its economy because of the dysfunction of all production capability. Additionally, the ability to ship by cargo ships came to a sudden halt. The general population no longer had reason to trust in a central government that intended to control everything. Civil unrest became widespread as the masses sought to survive. The same was true in Russia, where oil was the primary source of revenue. Now idled by lack of equipment and the means to ship it, the government had to turn to the people to expect agrarian means of generating life-sustaining resources.

The people, now aware that the government was weakened, turned to civil unrest to achieve freedoms they had lost. South America and Mexico, long ruled by family-affiliated centers of government filled with corruption and drug-related sources of revenue, found themselves without the means to keep their citizens controlled. In the Middle East, kingdoms were shaken for lack of devices that allowed them to live in splendor or by government subsidy. Unrest was prevalent, as freedoms were sought by people long subjugated to living on the edge.

The whole world was in disarray. The European Community nations influenced by socialist and communist factions came apart at the seams. The masses of immigrants from the Middle Eastern countries that had invaded Europe increased the burden on every individual as they all struggled to survive under the most difficult of circumstances. It would seem that no one could escape the hardships put upon all, and yet maybe people here, too, would come to the realization that godlessness can only bring hardship and suffering if mankind fails to heed his truth and abide by his law.

Whether in Africa, probably the poorest and the most corrupt dictator-ridden continent in the world, or Australia, a nation of wealth and modern conveniences, all suffered the catastrophe brought on by the EMP. Each suffered according to their dependency on technological devices and the materialistic existence many had come to believe in and rely upon.

CHAPTER 17

A Call to Action

It's two years now since the EMP hit the earth. Over that time, the people in the United States have existed according to their willingness to work with others in the pursuit of peace and harmony. But there still was no cohesive government to help the people organize into the structure of unity and purpose that was so sorely needed. Before the EMP, the country was so polarized that the political entities exploited their power for the benefit of their own party and not necessarily in the best interest of the citizenry. Now a great natural purge had taken place and a chastisement by providence that required a new beginning. To that end, *The Group* and their network of representatives in each state of the union were about to assemble for the purpose of establishing the government as intended by the originators of this great nation. Their guide was to be the *Articles of Reconciliation*, and their blueprint would be the still existent *Constitution of the United States* along with its *Bill of Rights*.

By now, a level of communication had established itself throughout the nation by way of railroad and rudimentary telegraphy means. Though there were those who were struggling to make the ways and means possible to recover what was lost technologically, the total destruction of so much made it impossible to recreate what was lost except through what would be a long and difficult process.

Nevertheless, representatives of committed members of *The Group* in each of the states were contacted and invited to a meeting that would be called *The New Continental Convention*, a union of citizens to plan the reestablishment of the government of the United States. This meeting would take place in Fredericksburg, Virginia, in what would be the two hundred fiftieth year since the creation of the nation in 1776. By their actions, they would invite the country to put forward nominees for a new president as well as new representatives and senators to form the new government and the rebuilding of a great nation. When they left this convention, they would go back to their states and establish the mechanisms necessary to put forward their candidates and elect through primary elections, new senators, congressmen, and a president and vice president of the United States as well as those public officials necessary to serve the needs of each state.

The New Continental Convention was to meet at a reconstructed town hall in Fredericksburg. Able to assemble five hundred representatives from the various states, the participants would be broken up into groups representing the three main sections of the United States—an Eastern group, Midwestern group, and a Western group. This seemed natural since each of these geographic areas had interest's peculiar to their section of the country. These areas would then select leaders from their particular group and who would then debate the various issues that were significant to the citizens of their part of the nation. Once issues were identified, representatives would then take them to a formal meeting of *The New Continental Convention* to implement a unified strategy to the reestablishment of government by and for the people. Then formal nominees would be selected to run for the various offices of government. A day of general election would be determined, and the organs of government would be reestablished.

And so, it came to pass that on a summer day in Fredericksburg, Virginia, in the year 2026, a new *Continental Convention* met to form a more perfect nation. The former President of the United States, Daniel Solomon, would have the opening presentation to open the convention. Stepping to the podium, he began, "As this country was coming into being our second president of the United States made this statement, 'Our Constitution was made only for a moral and religious people.' Religion is the only basis for good morals, and for that reason, we must return this nation back to the precepts of religion and the duties of our citizens toward their fellow man. For those of us who are Christians, the prayer that Jesus gave to us stated very clearly, 'Thy kingdom come, thy will be done, on earth as it is in heaven.'

"In the fifth century AD, St. Augustine said in one of his sermons, 'Bad times! Troublesome times! This is what people are saying. Let our lives be good and the times will be good. For we make our own times. Such as we are, such are the times. What can we do? Maybe we cannot convert the masses of people to a good life. But let the few who do hear live well. Let the few who live well endure the many who live badly.'

"And an excerpt from *The End of the Present World* by Fr. Charles Arminjon, P. 94, said, '*The works of man, whether they are good or bad, are not always isolated, transitory acts; more often, especially in the case of the leaders of nations and those who are invested with public authority, they continue to subsist after they are concluded, either in the memory of other men or in public acclaim, as a result of the consequences they have had and the scandal they have caused. Thus, at first sight, a particular, secret crime seems to be only a private, personal deed; but it becomes social on account of its effects. Certainly it is of faith that there is a particular judgment, and that every man, at the instant of his soul's departure from the body, appears before the tribunal of God to hear his eternal sentence pronounced. Yet this judgment cannot suffice, and it is essential that it should be followed by another public judgment, in which God will not examine the actions in isolation and taken in themselves, but will examine them in their effects upon other men, in the good or evil deriving from them for families and peoples—in a word, in the consequences they produced and which those who perpetrated them ought to have foreseen.*'

"We as a nation must be steadfast in the certain knowledge that God is the supreme leader of his kingdom, and we are part of it. Creating us in his image and likeness, he wants us to aspire to the love of neighbor as he loves us. We have just come through a devastating intergalactic event as another sign of God's disfavor with the acts of man. He could have destroyed us completely, but again, by his mercy, he is giving us another opportunity to abide by his law. It is now our mission to see that we live up to his law and build a better nation for ourselves and be an example to the world."

With that, Daniel Solomon ended his presentation. There was a resounding hail of support as the congregation of representatives clapped and yelled their enthusiasm. Daniel Solomon went on to be one of the next candidates for president of the United States. He won handily because of his identity as a former President and the nation's enthusiastic support of the movements' *Articles of Reconciliation*. The country would once again prove to the world that as they stood by their belief *In God We Trust*, America would once again rise as a more perfect nation.

APPENDIX

Articles and Acronyms

Articles of Reconciliation

The *Articles of Reconciliation* is the set of principles that the members of the American Traditional Party is to adopt to counter the abuses that has played into the American political system. It is designed to reconcile itself with the needs of the people of this great nation as originally intended by the founders of the country.

Article I: It is the intent of the party to apply all action according to a God-based moral standard.

Article II: Civil rights will be applied to all citizens regardless of race, color, creed, or religion from conception to natural death.

Article III: Equal rights will be our standard, regardless of gender.

Article IV: The basic unit of society is the family unit. Marriage between one man and one woman is necessary to maintain a safe, secure, and happy home life.

Article V: Religion is to be embraced as the moral foundation for our citizens. *In God We Trust* is our commitment to the Almighty that he is who we rely on for our existence and our hope.

Article VI: Socialism and communism are to be condemned for what they are, a godless philosophy that establishes a class of elites to manage the non-elites. It debases mankind to the level of objects and profits by rewarding an elite class at the expense of the non-elite.

Article VII: The right to bear arms is to be supported as a right of all citizens unless abused by deviant individuals.

Article VIII: Free enterprise is the mainstay of a thriving nation. Capitalism allows this freedom to exist.

Article IX: Education must be taught by qualified teachers, and social norms should be taught at home, not in the classroom. It is the right of every parent to choose where their child will go to school.

Article X: As a party, we will act as servants of the people. Those who do otherwise will be banned from the party.

Article XI: The Constitution is our standard for issuing policy in governance of our nation.

Article XII: Elected members of this party will serve as temporary office holders limited to two terms. Once leaving office, they will be considered again as nominees only after the equivalent of six consecutive years in the private sector.

Article XIII: America is to act as the gold standard of freedom to the world so that by our example, we may be seen by other sovereign countries as a nation to be emulated.

Article XIV: Financial support to a community of nations, only if they pay their fair share.

Article XV: Income taxation must be assessed at no more than 10 percent of net income. All other tax should be *ad valorem*.

Article XVI: It is the intent of this party that the country must be operated on a balanced budget basis. All departments must seek to operate within budget, and surplus should be rewarded to department employees based on a non-excessive bonus amount as a percentage of their annual salary. The remaining surplus balance must be carried forward to the next year's budget. Budget deficits will be calculated into the subsequent fiscal period and will be deducted from forecast objectives until a balanced condition is reached. Manipulation of budget forecasting for the purpose of personal or departmental gain will be forbidden and subject to immediate legal action.

Articles of Acquisition

The *Articles of Acquisition* is a mandate established by a *Committee* of elitists who intend to convert the United States of America from a free and democratic country to a socialist state where the selected elite control all aspects of this nation's people.

Article I: The end will justify the means whether or not traditionally amoral or immoral.

Article II: The growing civil rights movement will be exploited for the Party's own sake and not necessarily for the best interest of minorities or underprivileged. As a fact of history, give them what they can get for little or nothing, and they will obligate themselves to you. The general population will then support the Party because Americans love the underdog.

Article III: The growing feminist movement must be exploited. By supporting them, it will foster planned parenthood and abortion. By furthering a general acceptance among the population, it will diminish the need for family unity and further the goal of government involvement in child welfare and population control.

Article IV: Exploit the liberal establishment and their ideals. By promoting liberal attitudes, the general degradation of traditional moral concepts will pave the way for socialist involvement through government intervention.

Article V: Debase the religious right and particularly the Catholic Church. Socialism has no place for religion.

Article VI: Support gun control in all its forms. By placing weapons only in the hands of government authorities. Government strengthens its dominance over the citizenry.

Article VII: Support the unions, particularly the corrupt and mafia-influenced unions. They will become the enforcers in our new society. When all government agencies and all associated government departments are unionized, they will become the shakers and movers to bend the general population to the governments will.

Article VIII: Infiltrate the biggest businesses in the land. Seek out the corrupt, and encourage them to exploit these companies to the point where government must take them over. Start with the banks and mortgage lenders and then the key industrial corporations.

Article IX: Education is to be dominated by liberal educators so as to allow indoctrination of the tenets of a socialist system into the minds of our young people. It must start at government-controlled preschools and through the high schools. Colleges and universities that support liberal thinking should be encouraged so as to develop within the minds of their students socialist ideals. The liberal colleges, universities, and institutions should be the source of advisors, drawn from the academic staff to mentor our bureaucratic and political planners.

Article X: The media, as predominantly liberal, should be exploited so as to encourage biased reporting in all its forms. Through its vast reporting capability, it will act as a conciliatory voice to our cause and bring constant criticism to our adversaries. They have the power to turn the thinking of the population in our direction.

Article XI: The entertainment industry, long a liberal, and amoral industry must be encouraged to liberalize and further debase the population. By their degradation of family, family values, and by fostering sexual freedom in all its forms, they will make it easier to establish socialist controls when and where we want.

Article XII: Taxation should be maximized wherever and whenever possible as a matter of course. By creating a complex tax burden, the government always has the upper hand in assessing and spending. Since the bureaucrats and politicians control the use of funds, they can enrich themselves at the expense of the population and remain the elite.

Article XIII: The environmentalists must be exploited by encouraging them to exaggerate the effects of mankind on nature. By continually expounding on man's responsibility for the effects taking place with the changes in the environment, mankind takes the position that government is the only answer to man's destiny. Vast financial sums will be directed toward typically liberal environmental establishments who can then be persuaded to direct some of those resources to our cause.

ACRONYMS

ATP – American Traditional Party
C3P – Citizens' Progressive Populist Party
SCOTUS – Supreme Court of the United States
T2P – Technocratic Progressive Party
GSA – General Services Administration
NTSB – National Transportation Safety Board
EMP – Electromagnetic Pulse
ICBM – Intercontinental Ballistic Missile
ATM – Automatic Teller Machine
GPS – Global Positioning System
POTUS – President of the United States
FBI – Federal Bureau of Investigation

ABOUT THE AUTHOR

Walter E. Schmidt has written two books before this work. After graduating from college, he entered military service during the Vietnam era. After an honorable discharge as captain in the US Army, working in the insurance and aerospace electronics area, he started his own company. During his working career, he had three businesses, the last twenty-five years as a small business advisor to small- and medium-size companies. His experience exposed him to the successes and travails of this USA. He sees the perils that confront this nation if things go down the wrong path. Though confident in the resilience this nation has in meeting adversity, there is still hope that we will always be the freest nation on earth. This work is an eye-opener if we, as a nation, forget that Providence holds all the cards.

Printed in the USA
CPSIA information can be obtained
at www.ICGtesting.com
LVHW090341190924
791303LV00002B/151